Time For Me

First Edition Design Publishing
Sarasota, Florida USA

Time For Me
Copyright ©2014 Carissa Kopf

ISBN 978-1506-911-65-6 AMZ
ISBN 978-1622-879-47-2 PRINT
ISBN 978-1622-876-15-0 EBOOK

LCCN 2015943975

June 2014, 2024

Published and Distributed by
First Edition Design Publishing, Inc.
P.O. Box 20217, Sarasota, FL 34276-3217
www.firsteditiondesignpublishing.com

Acknowledgments

To my publisher, First Edition Design Publishing, thank you for all your advice and guidance.

To my proofreader, Karen Jonaitis, thank you for the magic you did with your red pen and for being so enthusiastic about my book.

A big thank you to all my friends at the Amateur Writers of Long Island group for listening and critiquing my chapters.

To the Chlupsas for the many weekends I spent at their home near the vineyards which inspired my story.

To my mother, Arlene and sister, Erica, I would like to offer special thanks for sharing time with me talking about my story and the helpful comments you gave.

To my father, Donald, you are the wind beneath my wings...infinity.

To all my friends, I would like to express my gratitude to my friends who saw me through this book, by provided support, talking things over, reading, offering comments, and assisting in the creation of this story.

To my husband Gene and brother Steven, I would like to thank you for your love and support.

To my wonderful daughter, Amanda, "Ani ohevet otach"

Always follow your dreams, they will come true.
You are my angel and my inspiration.

Time For Me

Written by
Carissa Kopf

Chapter One

Oh no, another ride in the packed elevator to the fifth floor.

As I waited for the doors to open, a short man with a ponytail had his nose in a baseball article on the back of The City Press newspaper. A lady in a suit three sizes too small was either talking to a rubber tree plant that was between the elevators or had a hands free device I couldn't see from the side. Another man, taller, was watching a spider dangle from the ceiling. I could have sworn I'd seen him blow on it as it swayed back and forth.

Great, the doors finally opened and like hungry scavengers we filed into the claustrophobic cube. I was squished up against the back wall, behind a man that must have eaten the entire donut cart that was in the lobby. The doors closed and it seemed like forever before the elevator climbed to my floor. Of course it had to stop for every lit button. People on and off, on and off, everyone dressed in business attire. *Wouldn't it be great if a memo went around saying we can all wear jeans and sneakers?* That would be heaven, as my heels were already killing me and I've only been in them less than an hour. I was daydreaming of a very casual dress day, '*bum day*'. I would call it. Suddenly, I felt my face cringe.

What's that smell?

I looked around at everyone.

Shit.

It had to be from the 'donut' man.

Why can't they make farts smell like donuts?

I tried to press my back up against the wall even more, but couldn't. I wanted so badly to smack his bald head and say, "Are you stupid or something? Can't you see we're in this box and can't get out?" I could see others trying to step away. I wanted to scream, *"Sure, move away while I am pinned back here, but the joke is on you! You can't go anywhere either!"* One man turned his head and looked at me. I wanted to say, *"You should be back here, you skinny, no good looking, toothpick, let me blow you over jerk.* "Thank heavens, my floor. "Excuse me, EXCUSE ME need to get off here." The moment I stepped foot on the gray multi colored rug, the doors closed behind me. I stood there and took a breath. It was better than the gas tank that's on its journey up.

The office smelled like a mix of roses and musk oil. The sign *RELAX* was hanging up on the wall above the glass receptionist desk. Surrounding the desk were dozens of perfume bottles that were all advertised in *Relax magazine.* Twenty years and the magazine is still going strong. Last year, I suggested adding historical facts to the magazine ads, and I was promoted from layout designer to head of The Publication Department.

"Good morning Madison, how are you?" Claire Rays asked, as I walked up to the receptionist desk. Her chocolate curls bounced along as her chest popped out of her dress. Her boobs make a big statement and always put smiles on a lot of our client's faces when they walk in.

"What a very nice dress you have on Claire."

"Thanks."

"Do I have any messages?" What I really wanted to say was, "*Claire Rays, give us a break, really? Just wear a scarf or turtle neck, we're not selling peep shows today.*"

"Well, let me see," she said as she pointed with her finger along the mail boxes. "Madison Taylor, Madison Taylor, yes, right here." She turned and reached for them. Damn, the ride in the elevator was more than enough excitement for me today and now my poor eyes, her big boobs matched her derriere. Hey, nothing wrong with a big backside, but when you can see the cottage cheese marks through the polyester dress, there has to be a law banning the use of polyester. Wait, no. She didn't. A thong? Someone better cover my mouth because my words are about to explode all over her. I quickly took a mint from her candy dish and shoved it into my mouth. My mother always said, "Don't talk with your mouth full!" I took my mail and walked away smiling.

I had to chuckle when I bypassed Devin Allen. He was holding a mirror making sure every black hair strand was in place and grinning to pick any seeds out of his pearly whites, from the half eaten bagel on his desk. If he had one more x chromosome, I think he would have been a woman. Devin has a way about himself that can persuade a client into buying space in the magazine.

"Hey girl, glad to see yah," he said as he leaned back in his chair and put his polished shoes up on his desk. "I have an interview for you. Too bad you weren't in yesterday afternoon, because I worked it again and got the Pearlman account. Mr. Pearlman was a tough cookie, but he bought two spots. Also, the *Tame and Wild* collection will be advertised in the Fall magazine."

I leaned over and high fived him. "Congratulations! Way to go, my friend. I'm happy you got that account. Email me his number and I'll set up the interview."

"Already sent."

"Thanks," I said as I walked to my office.

I nodded to Dylan Adams, one of my editors. He was busy typing and talking on the phone. He waved his hand to say, "Come here" and pointed to a tall stack of files. I looked at him with a look of, "oh no, those are not for me." He winked as he kept working. I would have made a move on him a long time ago but he's married and has three little ones. That's just how my luck has been going. They're either married or gay. I do, however, enjoy watching his blond curly hair, baby blues, kissed-by-the-sun skin, 'let me hold your tight ass' walk into my office every day. Jaylnn, my assistant, and I inhale his scent and dream of bathing in it as he passes by. Jaylnn shares the office with me due to lack of space on our floor. We get along really well and enjoy working together. One time we looked up Dylan on the internet because I heard that he once modeled swimsuits. We found a few pictures of him, printed them out, and taped them to the inside of our coat closet!

Finally, with my arms full of files, I entered my office and plopped them on top of other leftover work. I sat down and looked over to Jaylnn's desk.

"Are you in here somewhere? Jaylnn? Good morning?"

She looked up and said, "Morning."

I saw her puppy brown eyes between shaggy brown highlighted bangs, that I so badly wanted to pull back with the rest of her hair, into the bun she had. I always wondered what she would look like without the cat eye glasses.

"I need a cup of coffee. Do you want one?" she asked.

"Sure, thanks."

Chapter Two

The fax machine bin was spilling over with more bios from clients that couldn't make their appointments. The phone lights were all flashing and the layout department just delivered two boxes of advertisements for me to proof. "Why did Jennifer have to move? I feel like I will never get caught up with my own work, let alone all hers. I need a vacation."

"I'll get us strong coffee," Jaylnn said.

I watched her walk away and I just shook my head at her outfit. She had on red and brown checkered pants with a tan frilly button up sweater, a black thick large belt and shiny brown boots. It's June and she's dressed for the dead of winter. Yep, I love her.

Between the strong coffee and the dark chocolate I stashed away in the back of my draw, I had the caffeine boost I needed to get through most of the morning. It was eleven thirty when Brian Victor arrived for his interview. He was around fifty years old with a full head of silver hair and dressed to kill. He was charming to interview and I am sure his cologne, DarkNight, will do well for him. A mix of sandalwood and nutmeg surrounded my nose as I smelled it. On my second sniff, Brian told me how he came up with the idea for it. He was on a cruise in Paris and saw the Captain greeting his guests, who were dining with him for *Captain's Night*. Brian wanted to create a cologne that can be worn by men with power. He designed the bottle in black glass and engraved a sail ship on the front. The top was a ship wheel. Brian left a few samples with me as I walked him to the elevator.

When I got to my office, Jaylnn was looking through the menus.

"Lunch from Michow's?" she asked.

"Sure. Smell DarkNight. It's going to be a money maker."

"Wow that does smell really nice. Give a sample to Dylan so when he comes into our office, we can smile all day!"

We both laughed.

"I'll see if anyone else wants to order." She walked out.

I leaned back in my chair and stretched. I pulled my auburn curls up into a loose ponytail and closed my hazel eyes for a few seconds. Behind my lids I could see myself sitting on a Caribbean Island, sipping a frozen margarita while two golden bronze hunks wearing the smallest bathing suits fanned large palm leaves over my body.

"Hey, snap out of it girl or let me in your fantasy," Devin said as he picked up one of the samples and smelled it. "With that smile on your face I can tell you are thinking dirty."

"I was just resting my eyes, Devin."

"This is going to sell like crazy. Can I have this sample?"

"Sure."

"So, tell me about the fantasy? Tell me," he said as he sat down in the chair across from my desk.

"I was just taking a mental break."

"If they are like mine then it's a vacation somewhere far away from computers, phone and paperwork."

"Just think of a tropical island that is all yours with everything you ever wanted," I said.

"I would have a party every night and relax on the beach during the day," he said as he waved the bottle and headed for the door. "Keep playing the lotto girl and you never know."

I took my shoes off and walked around the office. Maybe I need to eat to get some energy. I looked in the mirror that was on the wall and said to myself, *I really need to go away and get this thirty five year old body to relax.* I wasn't in bad shape but I did have a few more extra pounds than I wanted, as I pinched my sides.

"Stop looking at yourself and let's order. I'm starving," Jaylnn said as she handed me the menu.

While we ate sushi and vegetable tempura, we talked about all the vacations we could take if we won lots of money. Forty minutes later, the empty food containers were in the garbage, we were back to work. I set up interviews and Jaylnn cleared most of her desk off.

"Madison, I'm heading to my sister's house out east by the wineries tomorrow and she has a small studio apartment attached to the back. It faces the inlet. I go there once in a while to get my thoughts together and because I can't afford to go anywhere else. Plus, it's her birthday and I'm taking her out for the day. You can come with me and have the studio to yourself."

"This weekend?" I asked.

"It'll be fun. Plus you said you need a break from all the craziness of life. You'll have shopping, wineries, the inlet, and no one to bother you there. Relaxation time! There are fields of grapes, fresh flowers, strawberry picking, and sunsets, instead of tall buildings blocking your view of everything."

"Okay, wine, sunset, and relaxation. Can we leave right now?"

We both laughed.

"Pack your bag and we can leave after work tomorrow," Jaylnn said.

"I'll pick you up in the morning so we don't have to leave a car here at work."

"Sounds good," she said.

As soon as I got home I opened my closet door and started pulling things out to pack. I took the copy of *Tiffany's Escape*, a romance story I have been reading for over a month, and swore to myself that I would finish this weekend. I even did my fingernails, toe nails, tweezed, shaved, and did a facial. You would think I was going out to a wedding or something, but this was my weekend away and I was thrilled.

At Seven thirty on the dot, Jaylnn was already sitting on her steps with her suitcase by her legs. I had to laugh once again. She was wearing a red skirt with yellow zigzag's, a white long sleeve silk pullover shirt and black heels. She put her suitcase on top of mine and we were at the office in twenty minutes.

I was so happy to beat the eight o'clock craziness in the elevator. I saw 'donut man' walking towards the elevator and I kept pressing the 'close door' button and right before he reached the doors, they closed. Oh this is going to be a great day! The morning flew by and Jaylnn and I were in my Mustang with the roof top down feeling the warm breeze surrounding us. The sky was a bright blue and not one cloud for miles. The sun took its time descending so night time was still hours away. We were singing to the song 'Smiling' by Steven James. Jaylnn changed into shorts and a tee while I drove, then I changed as she tried to steer from the passenger side. We laughed and giggled all the way there. Jaylnn told me about her sister and husband and how he was away on business, and that's why she was going there to keep her company on her birthday.

We took time to just enjoy the city disappearing into acres of green fields filled with flowers, and tons of vineyards. Ten minutes after I exited the expressway, I pulled into her driveway and parked on the side of the ranch style house. The front of the house looked like it was right out of a home decorating magazine, with perfect red painted shutters and grey vinyl on the front and sides. Flower beds were all around and a small wicker table and chairs were set off to the right of the lawn and a few rose bushes were in full bloom around the side fence. It was perfect.

Chapter Three

"It's been months since you've been here," Bella said as she walked up to the car to greet us.

"Madison," Jaylnn said, "This is my overly-annoying sister, Bella."

Before I could even say hello, she was hugging me.

"I'm so glad you took the ride. Jaylnn told me you needed a getaway. This is your place then. There are wine tours, pick your own fruit farms, restaurants, spas, and my favorite, lots of shopping!"

"Sold. I love this place already!"

Bella grabbed Jaylnn's arm and mine, and we walked up to the front door laughing, looking like we were multi-millionaires, with our heads up in the air, shoulders back, and hips wiggling from side to side. After the tour of the house we all decided to go out for dinner to celebrate Bella's birthday.

"Your house is beautiful," I said. "The backyard is breathtaking with all the flowers and the inlet. The water looks so calm. Like a mirror."

"At night, the houselights on the water look spectacular," Bella said. "It's perfect. That's one of the reasons we moved here."

"Tomorrow, you can explore all you want or just sit by the water," Jaylnn said. "Now, how does seafood sound for dinner?"

"Delicious!" Bella and I replied at the same time, laughing.

Over dinner, Jaylnn and Bella filled me in on all the spots to see and the best wineries to visit. We walked by the boats and then headed back to the house. I wanted to give them space for their sister bonding time so I excused myself after Bella gave me a key to the attached apartment in the back.

The place was decorated in a beach theme with blue and tan walls and ocean paintings displayed all over. What caught my eye was the coffee table. It was made to look like a Zen crystal garden. I knelt down and studied the forms that Bella or someone had created. The colors were breathtaking together, the way the blue and white crystals were positioned to look like the ocean waves cascading over the sand to forming an imitation of the beach.

After a quick shower and a cup of tea, I climbed into bed and picked up where I left off in *Tiffany's Escape*. *I should have finished this book a long time ago. How could I have put it down at this juicy part?*

> *Pushing her against the wall and touching her skin with his lips, trailing kisses down her neck, chest, and his tongue teasing her belly ring. Pulling the dangling heart with his teeth, he sent shivers straight down to her most sensitive spot. He continued south with kisses and licks until he was right above her mound. "Oh, Jaid, yes." Tiffany arched her back, and ran her fingers through his sandy colored waves. Pulling his head closer to her. Jaid could smell her sweet scent, but he wanted to tease her more, and hear her moans become needier and needier before he would fulfill her wishes. He grazed his hands up her thighs and gently blew on her . . . .*

What the, who is calling me at this time?

"Hello?"

"Hey Madison, Meyers Department Store is having a huge sale on everything and we can get some really great buys. Want to go with me tomorrow?"

"Mother, how are you?"

I closed the book and started fanning myself to stop the warm sensation I was feeling.

"Are you all right, dear? Did I wake you? Your voice sounds so low and groggy. Are you sick? "

I wanted to tell my mother that I was having mad passionate sex with my romance novel and was about to explode, when she called.

"No, Mom. I'm fine, just relaxing and watching the news before going to bed."

For the next half hour, I heard all about the sale, her lunch with Aunt Vicky and how Benny from the clubhouse won two hundred dollars at Bingo. With a promise to go to the sale during the week, we said our goodbyes. I plugged in the cell and turned it off. I continued reading the steamy chapter and was wondering what it would be like to have lips, licks and fingers all over. Oh how I miss the touch of a man. It's been too long.

I was awakened early the next morning by a boat motor starting. I wanted to run down to the water and yell, *WHAT THE HELL IS YOUR PROBLEM?* but when I opened the door, I couldn't believe what I saw. Something I didn't see in the city very often. The sky was a watercolor palette of oranges, pinks, reds, and yellows all blended together, pouring over the inlet, as the breeze took the colors into a slow dance on top of the water. I grabbed my camera, wrapped myself in a throw blanket, and headed out to take pictures. I sat on the edge of the small dock and snapped away, and then I laid back and watched the colors mingle in the sky. *Could all this be real? Do people really live like this? Could I live this way?*

After a cup of coffee and a granola bar, I showered and dressed, grabbed the keys, map, and cell phone then headed out the door. When I turned on my phone, there were three texts from work.

"Work, really?" I said out loud. "I can't even get away for a few days."

Text one, from Claire, "ur away but the Hillard acct called 3x, want the # txt me." The second was from Devin. "Hey girl did it again 2 more ads 4 Relax Mag. Files on ur desk, when r u coming back? Don't do anything I wouldn't ;) Miss u." The third was from Dylan, "I proofed the ads u left and r ready to go. I checked ur email box and u have 5 interviews 2 do set for wed, thurs, fri. txt me. Boob girl is making me crzy with ur mail. Ur D."

I'll get back to them later.

Chapter Four

I found Main Street and parked. I couldn't help but think about the office, so I texted Dylan. "Hey D, e me the info u got on the interviews, tell Claire 2 chill on the Hillard acct, I will deal later. Tell Devin lol and great job. Chat soon, M thx."

There were so many stores I had no idea which one I wanted to go in first. I passed a bakery with fancy cupcakes in the window, antique shops, and Mom and Pop eateries, but what got my attention was a bath shop. You could create your own bath products, like scented oils, rubs, soaps and lotions.

Oh, a nice bath to relax in tonight.

After creating a lavender scented bath set, I found a store called *Peaceful Moments* and my curiosity took me inside. I was in love. Every kind of crystal, rock, and shell that you needed for a Zen garden was in my sight. I strolled through the store and found starter kits. I grinned as I found one that was perfect for my living room. I even bought some separate crystals that were the colors of the sunrise this morning. The little old lady behind the counter put information about Zen gardens in the bag and told me to come back soon.

A few stores down, there was a restaurant called, *A Little More Stuffed.* My stomach started speaking in a low rumble. I walked in and I could see why the owner chose that name. The sandwiches were at least four inches tall and filled with whatever you wanted. I ordered turkey, bacon, and avocado with swiss on rye. While waiting for my order, I noticed the paintings on the walls of different wineries from years ago to the present time. That's when I decided to take my lunch to a winery and enjoy eating with a perfect view of the vineyard.

"Excuse me?" I asked a waitress walking by. "Is there a winery where I can enjoy a picnic on the grounds?"

"Sure. Most of them you can," she said. "Go to *ClearGrape* vineyards. It has the most wonderful sitting area and live music. When you're done eating, you can walk across the street to the farm stand.

They have the cutest little market you can stroll through and they make the best blueberry pie you'll ever taste. Tell Ann Marie that Sara sent you and she'll throw in a handful of her 'melt-in-your-mouth' Caramel Kisses. You can't eat just one!"

"Thanks, I'll stop by."

"No problem dear," she said as she picked up her tray of dirty dishes and walked towards the back.

Perfect. I looked at the map and found the winery to be a few miles down the road.

The door opened to the restaurant and a child's laughter caught my attention. I looked over to see a little boy about four in a full belly laugh while a man held him over his shoulder. When he lowered the blond, curly haired boy, my heart went a flutter. My eyes traveled over his tanned, muscular body up to his perfectly carved face. His ocean blue eyes made me weak in the knees. My trance was broken when I heard a woman's voice calling out.

"Bryce, leave him alone. You'll make him dizzy."

REALLY, he's married!

"Excuse me, Miss. Your order is ready up front," the counterman said. "Miss?"

"Oh, yes. Okay, thanks."

While I was in line to pay I felt something hit my sandal. There was a toy car at my feet. I looked around and the blond little cutie was looking at me. I squatted down and pushed the car back to him.

"Oh, I'm sorry. Cole, don't bother the lady," the man named Bryce said.

Even his voice is sexy.

"That's okay," I replied. "He's no bother!"

"Bryce," the woman called out. "Let Cole pick out his drink."

"It was nice playing cars with you, Cole," I said.

Smiling, Bryce said, "We better get going Cole. Say goodbye to…"

"Madison," I answered.

He extended his hand for mine and said, "I'm Bryce, nice to meet you, Madison."

I slid my hand into his.

"Nice to meet you too, Bryce."

"Enjoy your day," he said.

I watched him walk away with Cole.

As I drove to the winery, I noticed the shades on the street lamps were designed to look like clusters of grapes. It gave the street a nice look along with the fancy store fronts. When I pulled up to *ClearGrape*, the door handles were shaped like a wine bottle and a wine glass.

No wonder the streets were empty. Everyone was in the tasting room. Wine bottles were stacked from floor to ceiling, standing tables were all around and booths were against the back wall. A refrigerator the size of a large living room was set into the wall with glass doors showing off all the racks of bottles and a few wine barrels.

There were people standing around tasting, swishing, and looking through wine glasses that were filled with light and dark liquids. I found my way over to the bar and scanned the wine list. Taking my glass of Zinfandel, I headed out to the back vineyard. There was a pianist playing on the deck, tables filled with people in their own conversations, blankets spread out on the grass with families sitting, and frisbees being flown off to the side of the vineyards. I looked around and found two empty adirondack chairs in the distance, so I started to walk over to them when two teens plopped right down.

Really, come on. I just want to kick back and enjoy lunch.

Looking around again, I found no empty spots. *Well, I guess the step to the deck will have to do.* I sat down and was about to eat my sandwich when the teens got up and ran off through the vineyard. I jumped up and quickly scooted over to the chairs. I slipped off my sandals and sat back sipping my wine as I ate half of my sandwich. The music sounded so calming and the sun warmed my skin. I closed my eyes and felt the tension release from my body.

"Hello, Madison," Bryce said.

I sat up, knocking my wine glass off the arm rest of the chair, and saw my dream man standing in front of me.

"I think that fly is enjoying your sandwich," he said. Motioning to the chair, "May I?"

"Please," I said as I wrapped half the sandwich and shoved it back in the bag.

"Nice view," he said as he nodded his head towards the vineyard as he sat down. "It's so peaceful and beautiful."

"Yes, you're beautiful," I said in a whisper as I moved in my seat to face him.

We both reached over to pick up the glass and almost bumped heads.

In a low, sultry voice he said, "I think you have that wrong, Madison. You're beautiful."

Oh shit, he heard me.

Softly, I said, "Thank you."

"You look like you need another glass of wine as the grass drank it for you." He smiled. "What were you drinking?" He held the wine glass to his nose and sniffed it. "Zinfandel, maybe?"

How did he know?

"A wine connoisseur, are you?"

"Smells a little sweet and is rosy in color." Then, he dipped his finger into the little bit of wine and licked the liquid off it.

I thought I would die watching his tongue slide over his finger.

"Yes, a 2009 Valley of the Moon, Blush, I'd say, very nice choice Madison."

I looked at him questionably.

"I know a bit about wines," he said.

"You even know the year and name?"

"I like wines. Listen, *ClearGrape* is having a tasting tour tonight. Would you like to join me? It's by invitation only. *ClearGrape* created a few new wines and would like to get some feedback on them and you can vote for your favorite one. The winning wine will be featured in the *Pressman's Fine Wine* Magazine. Plus, everyone receives a complimentary bottle of their choice. Please join me?"

Chapter Five

Cole ran over to Bryce and jumped into his lap.

"Uncle Bryce, Mommy's getting ice cream!"

Uncle, YES! He's not married.

"Cole, say hello to Madison. Remember her from the deli? She rolled the car back to you."

"Hi," he said without turning his head. "Can we get ice cream? Come get some with me, Uncle Bryce. Please?"

"Okay, go back to mommy and I will be there in a minute."

Cole wrapped his arms around Bryce's neck and squeezed hard. "We're getting ice cream!" he said as he climbed off his lap and ran back to his mom.

"He always wants something. Please come tonight. It starts at eight," Bryce pleaded.

All I heard was eight as my mind was forming a sultry picture of his tongue sliding up, down, and around the ice cream cone.

"What do you say Madison? Can you make it?"

My eyes darted from his lips to his eyes as I realized I was fantasizing.

"Eight. Yes. I'll be there."

"Great. Would you like to get some ice cream with us?"

Only if you're laying down and it's melting on your hard, hot stomach.

"Umm, that's okay. Enjoy the time with your nephew. I'll see you tonight."

"I can't wait." He stood up and bent over, placing his hands on the wide arms of my chair and whispered, "I owe you a glass of wine, Madison." He placed a kiss on my cheek.

Before I could even think of something to say or gain control over my raging hormones, he was already trotting toward the blanket where Cole was waiting.

My phone rang, bringing me back to reality.

"Hi Jaylnn, how are you and Bella doing?"

"Oh Madison, we're having a wonderful time. We're shopping like crazy and found this store that has everything you need to dress up an outfit."

"Well, that's your type of store. You sure you don't own it?"

We both laughed.

"What are you doing? Did you go shopping or sit by the water?"

"A little bit of both. Right now, I am sitting at a winery having lunch. It's so nice. I met someone and let me tell you, he's hot. He invited me to a wine tasting."

"You go girl, that's great. Tell me about him."

"He's a dream and very sexy. I'll tell you more when you get back."

"Tell me *something*, Madison. Don't leave me hanging."

"You're funny. I'll tell you more later."

"Okay, Bella and I are going to spend the night at a hotel here and take the ferry back in the afternoon. So enjoy your night and don't do anything I wouldn't."

Laughing, I replied, "Me, do something out of my norm?"

"Madison, remember when we went to the conference in San Diego and you met Paul. I think that was his name. You both had eyes for each other throughout the day and into the dinner party. When I woke up your bed was still made and you had the same clothes on when you walked into our room at one in the afternoon. So be careful."

"Oh, Paul, the salesman. What was his last name?"

"See what I mean, Madison?"

"He had the most amazing brown bedroom eyes," I chuckled. "I'll be fine, Jaylnn. Have fun, and tell Bella hi for me. See you tomorrow."

"Okay, bye."

I sat for another half hour and just relaxed. Then, I headed to the car when I saw 'Ann Marie's Farm Stand', so I walked over. The fruits and vegetables looked nice and healthy and the flowers were bright and colorful. *No wonder why I love summer so much.*

Strolling through the fruit area I picked up some plums, peaches and as I went to put a bunch of grapes into my basket, a pink lily was lying there. I stood staring at it.

How did that get there?

I looked around, but saw no one near me.

Am I going crazy?

I picked up the flower and smelled it.

"Psst."

I turned and Bryce was leaning on the edge of the orange display. His lips curved into a sexy smile.

I smiled back and started to walk over to him.

"For you my lady," he said as he bowed towards me. All of a sudden, the whole orange display folded in and he and the oranges went down. It looked like little bouncing balls all around rolling in all different directions. Bryce was sprawled out on top of the fake grass that held the oranges.

I tried dodging each orange as they used my feet as a target so I shuffled like I was new at roller skating. He was hysterically laughing and almost to his feet when I went to help him up.

His laughter was contagious and I joined in with him. I tried to ask if he was okay, but I couldn't get all the words out. After a few minutes of trying to catch our breath, we noticed others around us laughing and helping to pick up the oranges. A few of the workers came over with crates and told the customers that they would take care of it.

"Are you alright?" I finally managed to ask.

Still laughing, he said, "Yes. I am going to have to tell my sister to order stronger stands. Thanks to the grass cushion I'm fine, but I think I have a few indentations of oranges on my butt."

Oh, let me see, let me see.

"Come on," he said taking my hand. "I'll show you around. Oh, wait." He stopped short, letting go of my hand and walked over to the basket I had dropped and picked up the lily. He handed it to me as he slid his hand back into mine.

A perfect fit. I feel like Cinderella with her prince.

We started to walk when a woman came running over.

"I heard that someone fell into the orange stand. I hope they're alright," she said as she was on her tippy toes trying to look past Bryce. "I don't see anyone hurt."

"It was me, Ann Marie," Bryce said. "I fell back onto the oranges."

She busted into a fit of laughter and we were all laughing again.

"I'm fine, thanks for asking Sis." He smiled. "This is Madison."

Still laughing, Ann Marie said, "Pleased to meet you, Madison. You better watch out if you're going to hang with my brother. He's clumsy."

"I will. This is a wonderful place you have here," I said looking around.

"Thank you. It took some doing but was well worth it. Bryce, make sure Madison gets a handful of my special treats. Matter of fact, give her two handfuls. She's going to need them if she spends the day with you." She winked at me and walked away.

Special treat, oh the caramel kisses, yes!

"I thought you were getting ice cream with your family?"

"We did. My sister sells ice cream in the back, by the play area. "Bryce took my hand. "Come, I'll show you around. Over here are the fruits, vegetables, plants and flowers. The back is the cold section, where the homemade cheeses and dips are. Do you like roasted corn?"

"Yes, with lots of butter."

"Here, you have the knick knacks, candles, pottery, dishes etc. Then through here, you have the best donut making machine in the world. You have to eat them as soon as they are made. They melt in your mouth. My brother-in-law is known for his apple pie donuts."

As we passed the donut machine, I had to laugh inside as it reminded me about the donut man back at work. I wonder what his favorite donut is. Well, probably all of them.

"Over here is the ice cream stand. Jason, this is Madison."

"Hey," Jason said.

"What would you like? A double scoop cone, chocolate fudge bar, or something else?" Bryce asked pointing to a poster stapled to a wooden stand. "Pick from here. It's on me."

"Oh, you're such a big spender," I smiled at him. "I would like a roasted corn, instead of ice cream."

"Sorry, Jason, no sale from us."

"No big deal to me," he said.

"You're such a salesman, Jason," Bryce replied.

Jason just rolled his eyes when we walked away and headed to the roasted corn booth. We passed the swings, a few slides, a dirt track with small kid size tractors to ride and a small corn maze.

"Wow, your sister and brother-in-law have quite a place here."

"Yes, they have had it for over seven years and have won a few different awards and contests in all different areas, from the biggest pumpkin grown to the best blueberry pies. They even do a Jell-O eating contest for the children. That's always fun to watch."

Oh, he is so down to earth and A FAMILY MAN, mm.

Chapter Six

"Let's go through the maze," he said.

As we were walking up to the entrance to the maze, a couple maybe in their seventies, were sitting on the bench in front of the swings holding hands. He was waving to a little boy about five swinging on the swing, more than likely his grandson. The woman watched us walk by and smiled at me. Maybe she was reminiscing when she was younger and in love.

I was jolted out of my daydream when I felt Bryce pull me closer to him when some children were running and not looking where they were going.

We weaved in and out of the maze and he continued to tell me about the farm stand and how the first two years were the hardest for his sister, as there were so many people selling the same thing. There weren't enough people stopping by and the fruit and vegetables went bad and they started to lose money. They began to think it was a bad investment until his sister took home some of the fruit and made pies for the family and everyone gobbled them up, and said she should sell them, and *boom,* she has been doing great ever since.

Just then, a few more kids ran by and Bryce was forced up against me. I couldn't move anywhere as my back was already touching the corn stalks. His hand still in mine, our eyes met and gently he pressed his lips on mine. His kiss was so tender. I could feel myself starting to fall backwards but he placed his other hand around to my lower back and held me up against him. Our kiss lasted no more than a moment, because we heard kids laughing and running in our direction again.

"I should have my sister hang a sign that says, NO RUNNING."

"Kids don't read signs."

"You're right. Come, we're almost to the end."

A few minutes later, we were out and taking a picture that was put into a cardboard frame saying, "You made it through Ann Marie's corn maze."

An elderly man with long silver braids, wearing a beaded necklace with a small dream catcher hanging off of it, and moccasins on his feet, handed Bryce the frame and smiled at me.

"Here you go," he said. "Happy couple!"

"Sani, this is Madison,"Bryce introduced me.

"Madison," Sani said smiling, "Now called, Mai, meaning flower of beauty."

Smiling back, I said "Thanks. Nice meeting you, too."

"Thanks, Sani," Bryce said.

"Anytime, Atsa."

"You know he is a wise man and always speaks the truth," Bryce said as we walked away. "He would tell us stories that I thought were just silly Native American tales when I was little, but my father told me, for all the time he has known him, he has never lied."

"What does Atsa, your name mean?"

"Soaring eagle. He gave me that name when I was a kid, for having a creative imagination."

Creative imagination, I like that.

"What type of tribe is he from?"

"The Navajos. He named Ann Marie, Johana, meaning sunny. She was always smiling and it melted his heart."

"Sani means?"

"Old one. I don't know why his parents gave him that name, but I think it means smart man too."

"I like how the Navajos name a person after their good traits."

"Yes. Here," he handed me the frame. "For you to keep."

Smiling at him, I said, "I love it."

"What do you want to do now?" he asked.

Giggling, I asked "Oh, please, oh, please can we go on the tractors?"

He laughed and put his arm around me. "Let's get some roasted corn."

While we were eating, he told me how he helped his sister design the corn maze and how his friends fixed up the cottage next to the farm for their home.

"I was admiring that cottage as I pulled up to the winery. I love the country look it has."

"Come on," he said.

"Where are we going?"

"To get you a special treat." Then he winked at me.

Oh, I wanted to just pull him back and plant a big juicy kiss on those perfect lips, but I had to almost run to keep up with him. The market was quite busy for the late afternoon and as we got to the counter, a line was halfway down the homemade jam aisle.

"Wait here."

I watched him walk through the crowd as he stopped a few times to say hello to people he knew. I realized how handsome he really is. I slowly caressed his body with my eyes not to miss an inch. I gazed from his muscular calves, to his thighs, then to his firm backside, which filled his cargo shorts just perfectly and his tee shirt fit like a gentle hug. When my eyes found his, I knew I had been busted. He caught me checking him out. He winked at me and smiled, then disappeared behind the counter.

I wandered around the market while waiting and I laughed to myself when I spotted the orange display.

I'll never forget that.

"Boo, here you go my lady," Bryce said as he bowed and held a red gift box in his opened hands.

"Thank you Sir."

"Open it."

"Okay." Inside was a red rose. The stem was cut off and laid ontop of a bunch of candy, wrapped in copper foil. I looked at him, and lifted the rose.

"Caramel kisses?" I asked.

"Yes, they're not formed into a kiss, but when you eat them your lips pucker the motion as your tongue twirls around it. Try one," he said.

I looked at him, trying to comprehend his description of eating the caramel gem.

Oh I am feeling so warm below.

I watched his fingers slide across the foil and peel back the paper. His skin grazing the velvety sweetness and before I knew it, he placed it in my mouth. When I met his eyes, he cleared his throat and licked his fingers.

"See, there you go. You're making the kissing motion."

"No, I'm not!"

He was right. I was feeling the silkiness of the chocolate on my tongue.

"This is delicious," I tried to say.

"I told you, you'd like them."

He unwrapped another and popped it into his mouth.

"I should get going if I am going to make it by 8," I said. "Thank you, Bryce, for a wonderful afternoon."

"My pleasure. I'll walk you back to your car."

I got into the car and rolled down the window. Bryce poked his head in and kissed me goodbye.

"I can't wait until tonight," he said, and tapped the roof and walked towards the winery doors.

All I could think about on the way back to Bella's was the kiss we shared in the corn maze.

Chapter Seven

It was six thirty when I showered, wrapped a towel around myself, and tried to figure out what to wear. I wanted to look and feel sexy tonight so I was grateful that I packed my blue satin halter dress, just in case we were going some place fancy. It will be perfect.

Forty five minutes later, I was walking into *ClearGrape*. I caught a glimpse of my reflection in the mirror as I passed the coat room and wow, I looked hot. My hair cascaded past my shoulders in bouncing curls, either I lost a few pounds in a day or this dress hid some of my excess fat, but it fit every curve nicely, and the beaded wedges matched perfectly. I was about to walk away and head into the tasting room when I noticed a shadow in the mirror that seemed to be right behind me. I quickly turned to see if anyone was there, but I was the only one by the mirror. I quickly walked away and entered the main lobby.

There were people mingling and waiters walking around with trays of assorted appetizers and wine glasses. There were a few rectangle tables covered in gold tablecloths with rows and rows of wine bottles on top of them. I passed a display of antique bottle openers and another of different bottle toppers.

I'll make a mental note to look at them later.

"Madison," Ann Marie said. "How are you? You look lovely."

"Thank you and you look lovely as well. I love the lavender color on you."

"Let's go into the tasting room. Bryce is going to make a speech."

Bryce, speech, about what?

When we walked into the tasting room the music seemed lower and everyone was eagerly waiting by the patio doors as Bryce stepped up onto a small platform, holding up his glass to everyone.

I'm confused, why would he need everyone's attention?

"Welcome to *ClearGrape*. I'm Bryce Stevens and thank you for coming. We are all here to sample the new wines and vote for your favorite."

He works here?

"*ClearGrape* has been up and running for over forty five years and my sister and I are so happy to keep it going for another forty five years."

There was a round of applause and when he raised his glass again, everyone quieted down.

He owns the winery?

"The winning wine will be highlighted in the *Pressman's Fine Wine* magazine. Please sample the wines and place your vote in the ballet boxes on the bar. Wine connoisseurs are walking around to explain the composition of each wine and answer any questions you might have. Everyone will receive a complimentary bottle of wine of your choice from tonight's selection. Please enjoy." He raised his glass and the room filled with applause again. After a moment, he spotted me standing in the back. His eyes lit up and his smile deepened as he made his way through the crowd towards me, shaking hands and giving hugs when he passed his guests.

"Madison, you look stunning," he said as he took my hand and brought it to his lips.

Oh my!

"Thank you and you look very handsome in a suit and tie."

"Thank you." He kissed my hand again. "Come." He took two glasses of wine off a waiter's tray and led me outside. We headed towards a gazebo that was set off to the left of the patio. Once there, we both sipped and then, Bryce took my glass and placed it down with his. He wrapped his arm around my waist and pulled me closer to him. Then, he took one of my hands in his and brought it up to his chest. "Dance with me Madison."

Crap, I hate dancing.

The band was playing a very mellow piece and with one look into his baby blues, he made me love dancing. Our bodies swayed in slow motion. His eyes were on mine, his lips were so close, and he smelled so good. Our lips met, romantically we shared the next few minutes embracing each other. I couldn't hold back, sliding my arms around him and my hands up the back of his neck I deepened the kiss. I felt his hands moving lower down my back and grab a handful of my dress just at the base of my backside. Breathing heavy we both opened our eyes as our kiss slowed and our lips parted.

"My Madison."

"Yes," I sighed.

We stayed in each other's arms for a few more minutes, just swaying to the music.

"Let's sit down and relax," he said. "I am so glad you are here."

"Pleasure is mine. You didn't tell me you owned a winery?"

"It was my parents. They passed in a car accident seven years ago. Ann Marie took over the business and I, at twenty five was still playing the field and doing my own thing. That's when the farm stand across the street went up for sale and Ann Marie's husband bought it. His family owned a farm in South Carolina, so he knew about farming. They invested some money and made it into what it is today."

"How did your sister handle both places?"

"She worked around the clock. That's when I realized my sister was going completely crazy between the two and I got my act together, took some business courses and wine making classes, and after two years, I took over the winery."

"I'm so sorry about your parents. I can tell you and your sister worked really hard here. Both the farm stand and the winery are beautiful."

He squeezed my hand.

I felt so drawn to him for not giving up on his family and making something of himself.

"What do you do, Madison?"

I explained my job and what I do. I told him about getting away from the stress of work and how relaxing it is here and how I tagged along with Jaylnn for the weekend.

"I'm so glad you did," he said. "I hope you make every weekend a getaway to here. There are a few companies that I buy supplies from that are in the city around Time Square."

"My office is a few minutes from there and I live twenty minutes uptown."

He smiled and pulled me into a hug.

Oh, his arms feel so good.

"Well, I guess a few trips to the city can't be so bad," he said as he nuzzled his nose in my hair.

I tilted my head and leaned in to him. We stayed this way for a while until we heard a lot of commotion. We both looked over to the patio and it looked like there was a crowd of people forming around the bar area.

"Something's going on," I said.

Grabbing my hand, he said, "Let's go."

Ann Marie screamed from the top step of the patio when she saw us, "Bryce, Bryce, there's a fight."

"Stay here," he said as we reached the patio.

He flew up the steps two at a time. I lost him when I got to the top.

As I got to the top step, I got that eerie feeling again of someone staring at me. I looked around and once more there was no one that looked misplaced. Most of them were interested in what was happening inside the growing crowd that was forming.

All of a sudden, I heard someone say, "Watch out, Bryce. He's got a broken bottle."

My heart skipped a few beats and I gasped for air. I pushed my way through the onlookers only to see arms swinging and punches landing. One man yelled, "She's my wife, you should have never touched her." The man with the broken bottle in his hand came down and struck Bryce, who had jumped in to break up the fight. I felt my mouth open but was unable to hear my voice scream, "NOOO."

Slowly the noise came up to full volume when reality set back in and I saw two giant muscle men grab the men who were fighting. One said to Bryce, "I have him." But Bryce still had him in his arms when he repeated himself. "BRYCE, I HAVE HIM."

He let go and the muscle men took both of them away. Looking through the crowd, I saw Bryce searching above everyone's heads.

"Bryce," I yelled. "Bryce." In a flash, he was at my side.

In an alarmed voice, he asked, "Are you okay?"

"You're worried about me? You're the one that's hurt."

The bruise below his right eye starting to swell and change colors, blood was smeared across his check and his shirt held a row of red droplets from a fresh cut.

"Come. Let's get you cleaned up. Where's the bathroom?"

"Are you okay?" Ann Marie asked as she made her way through the people. "You're bleeding."

"I'm fine."

"Go to the hospital," Ann Marie said. "You might need stitches. Let Madison take you. I'll take over here."

"I'm fine. Nothing a Band-Aid can't fix."

Chapter Eight

In the back of the kitchen Bryce sat on the counter and Ann Marie got the first aid box and emptied the contents on the counter. I could see she was very nervous. She was pushing everything aside with shaking hands. She searched for the Band-Aids and first-aid cream. Bryce looked at me and rolled his eyes.

"Ann Marie, I'm fine," he said to calm her. "It's just a flesh wound. It will heal in no time. There's a clean shirt hanging behind my office door, can you get it for me please?"

"Okay. You want a drink, shot or something?"

"No."

She walked out and one of the bouncers walked in.

"Mitchell," Bryce said as I was wiping the dried blood from around the cut.

"I have the bastard in the back room with Tyler. You want to see him? Oh excuse me, Miss."

"You're right, he is a bastard," I replied.

Bryce just cocked his head and looked at me. I raised my eyebrow at him and stared back.

Tyler must be the other giant bouncer.

"Mitchell, Madison. Madison, Mitchell. He's a good friend of mine and one of the best bouncers I could ever have."

Oh, then how come you got hurt instead of him?

"Here's the shirt, Bryce," Ann Marie said as she walked in. "Is there anything I can do for you?"

"Please see that everyone has a glass of wine and everything is moving along." He knew if he didn't send her out of the kitchen, she would pester him to go to the hospital.

"Yes, yes, of course, I will. Anything else you need? Should I call the police?"

"Mitchell will take care of it."

"Okay."

"Thanks," he said as she walked out.

"I spoke with the couple," Mitchell said. "The wife said that the drunken man asked her to dance. She said no, and that she was married but that didn't stop Mr. Pushy. He just kept pressing the issue and went to take her hand. The husband stepped in front of her and told him to back off. That's when all hell broke loose. The couple is hanging out in the private tasting room."

"See if the couple wants to press charges against him, then we will call the police. If not and they want to stay, let them."

"You should press charges against him," I interrupted.

"Just call him a cab."

"Sure." Mitchell smiled at me and left the kitchen.

"So doc, do you think I need stitches?" he asked as he started to take off his jacket, tie and shirt.

Oh my.

"No. It's a small cut." I said.

"Just put a Band-Aid on it and I'll show you around."

He groaned when I pulled the Band-Aid tight.

"I'm sorry, all done."

When he unbuttoned his shirt and took it off, I wanted to jump him and cover his chest with kisses and rub my finger nails softly along his skin. I tried really hard not to stare, so I watched from the corner of my eyes as I was refilling the first aid kit.

He's beautiful.

"Let me see how the couple is and then I will show you around."

"Okay, I'll put everything away here."

"Thanks, Madison."

I winked as he walked out.

I finished cleaning up and was drying my hands when he was back.

"Wow! That was fast."

"They were already at the bar sipping away. I apologized and offered a complimentary cheese platter and bottle of wine. They were fine about everything and just wanted to continue their night. They are celebrating their fifth anniversary."

"I'm glad they didn't want to get the police involved," I said.

"Yeah, me too. Mitchell told me, as I was walking to the tasting room, that they were okay with it all. Come, I'll show you around."

Heading out of the kitchen, we passed bathrooms, offices, and storage closets. Walking into the lobby, a few people came up to us and asked if he was okay. An older, short man, wearing a full three-piece suit, holding an unlit cigar between his fingers and a glass of white wine in the other hand, nudged Bryce's arm, "A little war injury to tell your grandchildren someday," he said, as he lifted the cigar pointing to Bryce's bandage and winked at me.

"Mr. Reyes. How are you?" Bryce answered patting the gentleman on the back and not letting go of my hand. "How's Mrs. Reyes doing?"

Laughing, he said, "Oh she's sampling all the wines over there." He pointed to the bar. "She is having a hard time picking one she likes, so she said she has to try them again."

We all laughed.

"So, who is this charming young lady you have here, Bryce?"

"This is Madison, my girlfriend."

Girlfriend, oh yes, I'll be your girlfriend, lover, wife, bearer of your children. Oh shit, what am I thinking? Girlfriend is nice. I smiled at Bryce.

"It's a pleasure to meet you, Madison."

"Mr. Reyes is the owner of the *Pressman Fine Wine* Magazine, which will be featuring the winning wine," Bryce said.

"That will be wonderful," I said. "I am sure an eight by ten would do the trick with a bio of Bryce and the history of the wine selected."

"You seem to know a little about advertising," Mr. Reyes said.

"Madison is the director of the publications department of The *Relax* Magazine in the city," Bryce explained

"Yes, a fine magazine for advertising perfumes and colognes. They are lucky to have you Madison. My wife enjoys reading the history of how the scents came about. When I looked through the magazine, I was impressed on the layout of the pages and agree with my wife about having a story behind the scent and design." Reaching in his pocket he pulled out a business card and handed it to me. In turn, I gave him one of mine. "Call me and we'll talk. Got to go and make sure Mrs.

Reyes is not voting too many times. You both take care now, and Madison, we'll talk."

"Enjoy your evening," Bryce said.

Looking at Bryce, I said, "WOW."

"You never know what a phone call can do," he said taking my hand. We went through the tasting room and everything was back to normal. Guests were conducting tastings, laughing, dancing and filling out their ballots. You would never know there was a fight a half hour ago. Even Mitchell and Tyler, the bouncers, were walking around this time a bit more focused. Passing the pictures on the hallway walls, I noticed one of a family standing next to the *ClearGrape* sign.

"Is this your family?"

"Yes."

He told me who each person was, and then he pointed to his parents.

"You look like your father, very handsome." He had broad shoulders, curly black hair with hints of gray on the sides. He stood a few inches taller than his mother. She had a wonderful big smile, long auburn wavy hair and very pretty blue eyes.

"Your parents produced a very attractive son," I said.

Then I felt a soft kiss on my shoulder and that was when I realized his arms were around my waist and my back was leaning on his chest.

Such a nice feeling.

Chapter Nine

"I want to show you something. Close your eyes." He took my hand and guided me through a door. I could smell a strong aroma of wine but it wasn't too over bearing. It was a sweet and fruity scent.

"Here, give me your other hand. There are six steps."

I took each step slowly and really wanted to open my eyes. *Maybe I shouldn't be doing this*, I thought. But I couldn't help myself. My curiosity took over.

"Okay, one more step. There. Keep your eyes closed and just walk with me."

"Are we in the cellar?"

"It's a surprise."

Hmm? Surprises can be very enticing.

"Just a few more steps, okay, right here, and don't move."

"Okay," I answered. But I didn't hear anything, just some clinking of glasses, some swooshing liquid, then silence.

"Are you peeking?"

I shut my eyes tighter.

"No."

I couldn't hear anything.

"Bryce?"

I started to open my eyes but before my lashes parted I heard him say in a low sexy voice, "I'm here."

I can feel the heat of his body next to mine, so close to me.

How did he do that? Please kiss me. Wait, what was that wet, chilled feeling on my lips, the smell of fruit surrounding my nose, is that his finger? Oh that warm feeling inside me began to stir.

He whispered, "Taste, Madison."

I opened my mouth slightly and he slid his finger a little deeper and automatically my lips closed around it, tasting the gift of the grapes. Oh, so sweet. I wanted to see his face, his eyes, and his finger in my mouth.

He replaced his finger with his mouth and we were kissing. Our arms were wrapped tightly around each other and we pressed our bodies together. He pulled slowly away from my lips but I slid my hand around to the back of his head and pulled him tighter to my mouth. He moaned and his hands caressed my bare shoulders and slid down my lower back pulling me to him. I could feel his enjoyment against me from our kiss. Lowering his lips to my chin, neck and shoulders, I whispered, "Please let me open my eyes? I want to see you."

"No, not yet, there's a blanket. Let's sit."

"Blanket?"

"Do you trust me?"

"Yes."

Slowly, he pulled my hand and guided me to sit down.

"I'm going to give you a private tasting," he said.

"Private?" *Oh yes!*

"Glass A," he said.

The aroma of citrus hit my nose first and a moment later, I felt a cool glass touch my lips. I tilted my head and sipped the crisp, fruity wine.

"Mmm, cool, crisp, fruity, I think lemon or lime twist, a white wine?" I licked my lips.

He didn't answer, all I could hear was another wine being poured into a glass and then I felt the coolness of the glass touch my lips again.

"Glass B," he said softly.

Again, the sweetness of the fruit coated my tongue. Strawberries, cherries, and then a taste I couldn't recognize lingered. I licked my lips to see if I could taste it again. I heard Bryce moan slightly.

Oh, he's watching me lick my lips. I traced my tongue over my lips again to tease and even though I couldn't see, I heard his breath quicken. *Oh, this is so much fun.*

"That's a red. It's delicious."

"Okay, take a bite of this cracker to clean your palette," he said, and I felt the cracker slide into my mouth and his fingers trace my lips. I shuddered from the feeling.

In a teasing voice, he asked, "Are you cold, Madison?"

"Umm, no, no I'm fine."

Bryce Stevens, I am going to tease you so bad.

"Glass C."

When he put the glass to my lips, I inhaled slowly allowing my chest to rise. I arched my back slightly knowing that my halter dress was already revealing my cleavage and by this small, sultry movement I knew he could see a bit more.

I knew it worked when I heard him moan and a glass fall over.

In a calming and innocent voice, I asked, "Is everything alright? Can I help you?"

"NO. Don't open your eyes." Clearing his throat he said, "Everything is fine, glass C."

I opened my mouth even before he was going to give me a sip. I moved my lips in a slow wanting motion knowing he is watching, but there was no wonderful scent or wetness touching my lips.

"Bryce, glass C?"

"Yes, yes glass C."

All of a sudden I felt his lips on mine and a slight moan escaped from my mouth. I felt his hand slide on my cheek to the back of my head pulling at my hair so gently, that it made my head tilt back. I felt his lips touch mine and he parted his lips and the wine flowed into my mouth. Drinking from him, every erotic sensual part of my body came alive. The flavor of apricot and orange invaded my mouth. It took everything in my power not to open my eyes and make mad passionate love to him.

"More, please."

I heard him chuckle, and the sound of pouring again.

"Ready for glass D?" He asked.

"I already made up my mind and I like the one you just gave…," but another glass was to my lips before I could finish the sentence.

A very sweet wine was wetting my lips, a bit too sweet, chocolate lingered on my tongue. "A red dessert wine I think."

"Taste test is over, but one more thing before you open your eyes."

"What?"

"Lay back."

Oh my.

I lowered myself back, feeling Bryce's arm at mine lying next to me. *What is he up too?*

"Okay open your eyes."

I blinked a few times and when my focus became clear, I was amazed. We were surrounded by huge silver vats, about ten of them. *I knew we were in the cellar.* There was a label printer against the far wall where the stairs I came down were. I turned my head and to the side of the blanket was the tray of wine glasses, a vase with one red rose and a dish of crackers.

"You like?" He whispered.

"Yes, very much," I turned to look at him. "When did you…"

His lips were on mine and we shared another tender kiss.

"Oh, Madison," I heard through his lips.

Chapter Ten

We both couldn't hold back anymore. Our bodies pressed into each other. Our eyes met and we knew we wanted more than a kiss. We wanted each other and I didn't care if I only knew him less than twenty four hours. I knew I loved everything about him and thought he felt the same way. Our kiss deepened and we moaned together. Our hands explored every curve and bump of each other's bodies and before we knew it we were both undressed and wrapped in the blanket touching, kissing and tasting what we both craved. Our movements were perfect and in rhythm with each other, in and out, in and out, picking up the pace when needed and slowing down to make the feeling last longer. I wanted every inch of him within me so I wrapped my legs around him, higher, his body pressing harder on to me. We could barely catch our breath. Then, with a final thrust, we convulsed in each other's arms. With his head on my chest, and my fingers still in his hair, we laid together savoring the moment.

In a faint voice, he said, "I want you, Madison." His warm breath on my breast as he spoke made me tingle inside all over again.

"Yes," I answered. "I feel the same. I came this weekend to get away from my crazy life and relax. I didn't know I would fall in ..." I stopped talking as he placed his lips on mine and kissed me softly.

Was it too soon to tell him, that I love him? I just met him, how do you fall in love in one day.

"Me too. I love you, Madison."

He loves me, yes.

"You have to vote. Come on," He said. He put his pants on and stood up. He helped me up and handed my dress to me. "These are for me."

He put my lace panties into his pocket.

I looked at him and said, "You're keeping my panties?"

"Yes."

Oh my, that's hot.

As we finished getting dressed, he asked, "Which wine did you like the best?"

The wine glasses were still in a row so I picked up the third one and took a sip.

Yes, this was the wine that was in his mouth as we kissed.

I took a sip and walked over to him. He was putting his shoes on when I slid onto his lap and took his face into my hands. I pressed my lips onto his and let the wine flow.

After a passionate kiss, I said. "This is the winning wine."

"Thank you." He moved me off his lap and stood. "You sit and I will tell you about the wines."

"No need too." I picked up the third glass again. "Just tell me about this one."

He took a sip and smiled. "Yes, a lighter white wine, symphony of floral aromatics, created by yours truly. It's called Summer Breeze. Made with apricots, oranges and a touch of rose water and blended with young green grapes."

"It's perfect," I said taking the wine glass and drinking the rest.

"We have to get back to the party," he said, taking my hand. We headed to the steps. "Do you know how sexy you are?"

"Me? You're the one with my panties in your pocket. Are you going to give them back?"

"No."

"What are you going to do with them?"

Before opening the door, he whispered. "Savor the scent," He chuckled and patted his pocket.

Another wave of warm feeling sailed through my body.

I didn't even have a chance to reply as he escorted me through the hallway into the tasting room.

The room was still filled with people. I excused myself and went to the ladies room.

What have you done Madison?

Looking in the mirror at myself, I smiled. I touched up my makeup and fixed my hair. *It's true, fooling around gives you a glow, or is it because I have no panties on?* My smile deepened.

Walking through the tasting room, I couldn't find Bryce. I went out to the patio and people were spread out all over. Trays of appetizers and wine glasses were being served. I took another wine glass from the Summer Breeze tray and took a sip, letting the wine linger in my mouth so I could taste each flavor. Off to the side I could see Ann Marie and another woman starting to sort the ballots.

The slightly cool breeze felt good and the stars sparkled in the sky. The moon was high, so it had to be around midnight or so. I looked at my cell and it was eleven forty five and I had four texts. I didn't bother looking at them. The night was perfect and I didn't want to deal with work or anything right now.

Where's Bryce?

"Excuse me." A tapping of a spoon on a wine bottle was heard through the microphone.

There he is looking so handsome, with his hair messed from, well... I had to grin.

"It is wonderful seeing all of you here. I hope you're enjoying your evening and have voted for your favorite wine. There is still time to vote if you haven't. Thank you."

A round of applause was given and wine glasses were raised in the air. Bryce had a full ear to ear smile on his face.

I raised my wine glass to him and he slid his hand into his pocket as he headed over to me.

He's holding my panties and no one but me knows. That warm feeling is back.

While walking towards me he took his hand out of his pocket and brought his fingers up to his nose.

Oh my, I love this man.

When he reached me he placed a kiss on my cheek and whispered, "Smells better than wine."

Blushing and trying to control running my fingers over his body right here in front of all these people, I said, "I can't believe there are so many people still here."

"Ah, don't try to change the topic. It will be my favorite scent from now on."

His wicked smile was so intoxicating.

I batted my eyes at him.

"Yes, my family and friends are wonderful to me and have been very supportive," he said as Ann Marie walked up to us.

"Hi Madison, how are you? Are you enjoying the evening? Is my crazy brother treating you well?"

Oh, you have no idea how crazy he is, private tasting, making love in the cellar, my panties in his pocket. Oh, he's treating me really well.

"It has been a wonderful night and yes, he is a gentleman."

"You let me know if he's not." She shot him a look and said, "Or he'll have to deal with me."

"Oh, I'm shaking, Sis."

We all laughed.

"Mr. and Mrs. Loris are leaving and wanted to place a large order of the Merlot for their restaurant," she said.

"Really, that's great. Have Mitchell take the order and set up a delivery date."

"I already told them I would be happy to help, but they wanted to talk with you. I think Mrs. Loris likes your charm," she said as she winked at us.

He looked at me, leaned over and placed a kiss on my cheek. "You have competition from a sixty five year old Greek woman. Be back in a flash."

"I'm jealous," I said as he walked away.

Chapter Eleven

"Madison, are you hungry?" Ann Marie asked.

"Starving."

"Let's get some munchies and go to the gazebo."

While we ate, she told me more about the farm and I told her about the magazine I work for.

"There you two are," Bryce said.

He was holding a bottle of Summer Breeze and some wine glasses. He poured and passed a glass to me, then to Ann Marie. He clicked our glasses with the neck of the bottle and said as he looked at me, "To a wonderful night."

"We're just taking a break," Ann Marie said, "And pigging out. How are the Loris' doing?"

"Good." They placed a big order for the Merlot and I sold them a few cases of the Summer Breeze too."

"Nice," Ann Marie said. "I should be getting back. You two enjoy this wonderful weather. See you inside." She tapped my knee and then gave Bryce a kiss on his cheek and walked away.

"I'm happy your wine tasting was a big hit," I said.

With a twinkle in his eye, he said, "How happy are you?" While he rubbed his fingers over my shoulder and down the middle of my back, I felt my insides heat up again.

I want him right now. I slid my hand down his chest, belly and right onto his forming bulge.

With a seductive look, I said, "Very happy!"

I pushed him back and he fumbled onto the bench. Lifting my dress a little to show my thighs, I straddled his lap.

"Madison!"

"The only thing that is stopping you from being inside me is your zipper."

"Well! Let me help you then."

Within a few moments, he was sliding into me. We both let out moans and we couldn't stop moving back and forth. His hands were under my dress squeezing my flesh as I clawed at his back. Our breathing quickened and became heavy. I pushed harder on him, wanting to feel every inch of him deep inside me, and with one swift motion, I was lying on the bench. My dress was above my waist and one leg was over the railing, the other on his shoulder and again he thrust deeper and deeper. Grabbing his arms I pulled myself closer onto him, making him moan even more. He and I moved together perfectly, faster and faster, matching each other's moan after moan, until we trembled with pleasure, feeling each other's explosion.

Laying on the bench our breathing came to a normal pace. I wanted to stay like this forever. With the music played in the background, the stars above, and Bryce on top of me. It was perfect.

Bryce started to get up, but I placed my hands on his face to stop him.

"This night has been so wonderful," I said. "I'm so happy I've met you."

"Does this mean you are my girlfriend?"

I'll be your girlfriend, wife or sex slave.

"Yes."

He went to say something but got interrupted by Ann Marie's voice over the loud speaker. "Ladies and Gentlemen, please hand in your ballots. There are five minutes left until we know the winning wine. Bryce Stevens, please come to the tasting room."

"Crap," he said. "You made my heart sing. I thought it never would."

Never?

"Come," he said as he stood up and helped me to my feet. "We should be getting back before the National Guard comes looking for us."

We fixed ourselves and started to walk back to the patio.

I had to ask, "Who broke your heart?"

"What?"

"You mentioned something about your heart never singing again."

"I was engaged a year ago and thought she was in love with me but all she wanted was the business. I was too stupid to realize it. The first time I showed her the vineyard she wanted to redecorate. She asked questions about the books, how much money came in and went out. It wasn't until I noticed the stock not matching the inventory printout and money missing from the deposits." We were almost to the patio when we stopped walking and he ran his hand through his hair. "She was stealing from me."

"I'm sorry that happened."

"I won't lie to you, Madison. I really thought I was in love with her. After I found out it was her, I broke it off."

I wrapped my arms around him and held him.

"I told myself not to trust again, but when I met you, it felt right."

"You can trust me Bryce."

The embrace lasted no more than a minute as we heard lots of clapping. We headed to the tasting room and there was Ann Marie and Mr. Reyes standing by the microphone.

"Ladies and Gentleman," Ann Marie said, "I would like to introduce you to the president and owner of the *Pressman's Fine Wine* Magazine where the winning wine will be advertised. Please welcome with me, Mr. Michael Reyes."

There was a round of applause.

"Thank you," he said into the microphone. "Thank you."

As the crowd quieted, he continued.

"I am very happy and honored to announce the winning wine. Bryce Stevens, please join us up here."

Another round of applause was heard. Bryce walked up to the platform with me in tow. I tried to pull away so he can have this moment with his sister but he tightened his grip on my hand.

Watching everyone gathering, seeing how happy they were to share in his moment, made me realize how happy I really felt for him and how comfortable I felt with him.

For a moment that feeling came back that I was being watched. I know people were looking at us, but the feeling I had was like daggers being thrown at me. I scanned the faces of everyone and they all were smiling and seemed to be having a wonderful time. Then I saw this woman, standing in the middle of the crowd, swaying back and forth, drinking from a bottle. Her eyes were dark and mean and she looked angry like she was about to lose her mind.

Doesn't anyone see her?

I looked at the people around her and some were involved in their own conversations, some sipping wine or had their backs to her.

Who is that person? Why is she staring at me? Why does it feel like we're the only two people in the room? Does she know me? Wait, does she know Bryce?

I started to shake.

Bryce looked at me and pulled me closer to him. He leaned over and asked, "Are you okay? You look like you saw a ghost."

I think I did, or an angry zombie.

"Madison?" He said. "Do you want to sit down?"

"No, no, I am fine. Please keep going."

Bryce turned to shake Mr. Reyes hand and I looked back to see the woman again but she was gone.

"The winning wine is," Mr. Reyes said as he pulled out the label, "Summer Breeze."

I felt like I didn't even hear the huge round of applause or the hugs from Bryce and Ann Marie.

Who is she and why is she staring at me?

I wanted to go over and shake her back to reality or tell her to take a picture, it'll last longer.

Then I felt Bryce's lips on mine. I snapped out of my isolated concern.

"What is it Madison?"

I didn't want to ruin the night by telling him what I saw. It could have been nothing. Just my imagination running wild.

"Your wine won," I said to him. "It's wonderful. I am so happy for you."

All of a sudden there was the sound of glass being shattered. All heads turned toward the table that held pyramids of filled wine glasses. It was her. She was smashing the pyramids down and the glass was shattered all over.

Bryce pulled me in close to him when we heard the glass shattering.

She screamed, "Bryce, you should be mine!" Her black curls looked like she had dipped her head into a pot of oil and were hanging in her face. Her dress, from what I could see, looked worn out and in need of major ironing.

Oh no, she's his ex?

She continued screaming. "This should be mine!" She flung her arms up and motioned to the building. "All of this." Pointing her finger at me, she continued, "You think you can come in and take it away, you bitch. I've seen you two out there!" She flung her arm in the direction of the gazebo and some liquid came out of the bottle she had in her hand like a volcano, and landed on a guest. "Tell her Bryce. Bryce, tell her you are mine, MINE."

"STEPHANIE!" Bryce said, forgetting the microphone was there. "IT'S OVER!" Then he realized how loud he was and stepped aside.

In a lower pleading voice, she said, "I need you. I'm a mess without you." Anyone could see she was totally out of it. She took two steps and fell. Bryce let go of me and went to her. Half way he stopped and looked back at me.

"You're the one," he said as he pointed to me. "Remember that."

Then he helped her up as she cried in his arms. I couldn't watch. I left and went out to the gazebo. I really wanted to go home, well back to Bella's place, but I knew I couldn't drive. I was shaking like crazy.

She was watching. How much did she see? Did she see us making love? She had to have been drinking before she came. The bottle she was holding didn't look like a wine bottle. Did she drive drunk? She could have died, well, what am I thinking? Stop it Madison. Bryce said he loves me and if it's true, then he will straighten all this out. I closed my eyes and let the tears fall.

Chapter Twelve

"Oh, I am so happy you didn't leave, Madison," Bryce said, as he was stepping up into the gazebo. "I thought after what happened in there, you'd be long gone and I would never see you again. I'm sorry you had to see that. Stephanie took it hard when we broke up and has issues with goodbyes."

"You think?" I asked.

"Hey." He placed his finger under my chin and lifted my head up. "She's nothing to cry over."

"What happens now? She wants you back?"

"It's the alcohol talking. I've never seen her so drunk. She's passed out on the couch and probably won't remember anything in the morning. She'll have a major headache and will apologize left and right when I see her again."

"See her again?"

"Don't worry. I'm not interested in her. Believe me."

"You went to her when she fell. Mitchell could have gone."

"I had to. Everyone was watching and I didn't want any more of a scene. I want you, Madison. I fell in love with you."

He took my hands and brought them to his lips and kissed them.

I wanted so bad to believe him and I knew I should, but this whole day was too much to take in all at once.

"It's late. I should be going. Plus, you have a few guests still here."

"Mitchell can handle everything. I'll take you home."

"He'll take care of maniac Stephanie, how?"

"Don't worry. He'll make sure she gets home in one piece."

Why am I even asking? I don't care.

"Come on." We headed back to the patio. "I have to grab a few things and talk to Mitchell, and then we'll be on our way."

"Okay."

I went to the bathroom and when I came out, Bryce was leaning up against the wall with an overnight bag hanging from his shoulder.

He's sleeping over?

"See you tomorrow, Mitch," Bryce said.

"Yep. Night, Madison," Mitchell said from the bar.

"Night."

I pointed to the bag and looked at him. With a grin on his face, he put his arm around me and we walked out the door.

He really loves me.

In-between giving directions to Bella's, we made plans for him to come and stay over next weekend.

When we got to the apartment, Bryce used the bathroom and I went to find something better to sleep in than a t-shirt and shorts.

"Here, wear this," he said.

When I turned around he threw his button down shirt on the bed and all he had on were pajama pants that were inches below his belly button. He looks so good.

Right where I was standing, I untied the bow at the back of my neck that held my dress up, and let it fall to the floor. Swaying my hips and teasing him, I walked to the bed and reached for the shirt. I didn't even have a chance. I was pushed down on top of it. His tongue tracing down my back while he separated my legs with his, then he lifted my hips. Feeling all of him within me made me want so much more. I pushed on him harder with every thrust he gave me until we both cried out for each other. His hands, fingers, and bites were like magic leaving me dazed and exhausted.

We could barely catch our breath when we collapsed on the bed. All I could remember as my eyes closed was the blanket being pulled up over my shoulders and Bryce's arm pulling me closer to him.

Chapter Thirteen

I woke to the sun beaming through the slightly parted blinds and the smell of bacon and coffee. I dragged my body out of bed and went to the bathroom, brushed my teeth, slipped on his shirt, and followed the smell into the kitchen.

"Hey there, sleeping beauty. It's about time you woke up."

I looked at the clock.

"Ten o'clock not's so bad." Then I kissed his cheek while he was scooping eggs onto a plate.

He laughed.

I poured the coffee for both of us, and he put the plates on the table.

"So, what are we doing today?" he asked.

We, nice.

"Jaylnn and Bella are heading back on the three o'clock ferry. They'll be here around four thirty, and then we are heading back to the city."

"Do you have to go?" he asked as he raised his eyebrow and tilted his head.

"I don't want to, but yes."

"Well then, we have to make every moment count. Eat up. I'll clean up while you get ready. I want to get you something to remember our weekend."

Smiling I said, "Don't worry, I'll never forget this weekend. Plus you have a souvenir of mine."

He looked at me and that wicked grin was back on his face as he patted his pocket.

I looked at him curiously and asked, "You have my panties in your pocket again?"

He pulled them out to show me.

I sat back, exhaled, and shook my head back.

He chuckled then downed the rest of his coffee as he shoved them back in his pocket.

A half hour later, I was in jean shorts and a lace tank. I gave my hair a quick blow dry, applied a little blush, then threw most of my things into the suitcase.

"Do you always pack that way?" Bryce asked as he was leaning against the door frame.

"Yep, ready to go."

We parked across the street from the deli were we met and walked hand in hand down Main Street.

"Here, we are," Bryce said, as he held the door open to Ava's Boutique Shop.

I stepped inside and there were shelves filled with various things from handmade vases to sculptures made out of utensils. I heard a husky man's voice say, "Morning both of you." I looked over at the counter and saw a tall white haired man with a full handlebar mustache. He was wearing a blue t-shirt, leather vest and jeans. His neck had a tattoo of a woman's face and there were different ink designs all over his arms.

"Hey there, Bryce man. Is that you? What's going on?"

They know each other?

"Hey there, Keg. How are you doing, old man?" Bryce answered.

"I'll show you old. Get over here you rug rat."

Keg? I think he got his name from his stomach looking like he swallowed a beer keg.

They clasped hands and gave each other a body bumping hug.

"Is my name still on the board?"

"Yep, you're still number one, the fastest Jell-O- shot shooter for four years now."

"If anyone wants to compete against me," he said as he tapped his chest, "they will have to down fifty two, no wait, fifty three to kick my ass!"

"Keg used to be my representative for a bar and restaurant supplier I dealt with," Bryce said. "Every time he would come by we would end up sitting and creating different wine concoctions. One day we thought of Zinfandel wine Jell-o-shots and there you go, we came up with fifteen different types of shots. We even tried beer ones but that didn't come out too well."

"After making them, of course we had to taste them and then we couldn't stop, so it became a challenge one for one," Keg said.

"How did you even walk after all that?" I asked.

Keg rubbed his belly and said, "I can hold a lot."

We all laughed.

"Where is Ava?" Bryce asked.

"She's visiting her mother this weekend."

"So you're on store detail?"

Keg rolled his eyes and smirked.

"So who's this fine-looking woman you have here?"

With a smile, Bryce answered, "This is Madison."

Keg extended his hand for mine.

"How you doing Madison?" he asked as he brought my hand to his lips and kissed it.

After a moment of being surprised, I said, "I'm good, thank you."

I looked at Bryce and he winked back.

"So what are you two looking for?" He asked while walking back to the counter.

Is that slippers he's wearing?

I looked again and I had to chuckle inside. This man's all dressed up in biker clothes and marked up in ink, wearing slippers and taking care of his wife's store.

"We're here to find a keepsake for Madison."

"Keepsake?" With his arms open wide he motioned around the store. "We got what you need somewhere here. I'll give you a deal too. Madison, take your pretty little self and look around."

Smiling, I said, "Thanks."

"If I didn't have my ball and chain on," I heard Keg tell Bryce, "you would have to watch out. With a little more wax on these handlebars, I would steal her from you."

I had to laugh inside. *Those handlebars would have been cut off in your sleep.*

I passed a shelf with handmade soaps and lotions, then a shelf with knitted scarves, another with painted teapots, animal banks, knitted baby caps and socks. Something told me this was a consignment boutique.

As I looked at the little gem boxes, I heard Keg telling Bryce that he had jewelry and my hearing zoomed right into what they were saying.

"Here's some earrings, necklaces, oh wait," Keg chuckled. "Looky here, handcuff charm."

"Keg!" I heard Bryce say.

"A little bit of excitement, man, for you two." I wanted to burst out with laughter not only because it was a handcuff charm, but because you have a seventy something year old man that is still sharp with his thoughts.

I heard Bryce say, "This piece here, I want that gold one."

Keg said, "Perfect for you two."

I stepped closer so I could maybe see what it was but I couldn't. I just heard Keg tell Bryce to give him forty. But Bryce said it was worth more than that and Bryce said he was going to give him eighty.

I was holding a little green gemstone jewelry box when Bryce rested his chin on my shoulder. He wrapped his arms around my waist and said, "Thaaat's prreettyy."

I giggled and held it up to the light.

"It reminds me of the winery and the color of the vineyard."

I felt a kiss on my cheek, and then he said, "Maybe you can put this in it while you sleep."

"Oh, it's beautiful." I turned in his arms and kissed him. "A bracelet, with a dangling wine glass charm, it's perfect."

"Like you, baby."

"Thank you, Bryce."

"You're welcome. Come, let's get going."

Bryce bought the box, and we said our goodbyes.

Chapter Fourteen

We stopped by to get Bryce's truck on the way back to Bella's and then sat by the water to eat the sandwiches we picked up. As we relaxed, the warm breeze hugged our skin and my thoughts drifted to possibly moving here. I imagined looking out over a lake or a vineyard every day when walking out my front door or opening my blinds in the morning. It beats the big buildings and busy streets of the city.

"You look a million miles away. What are you thinking about?" Bryce asked.

I went to answer, but Bella pulled up and I heard Jaylnn yelling.

"Madison. Hey Madison, we're back."

"Come," I said to Bryce. "I'll introduce you."

"Hey girl, I missed you." She looked over at Bryce, smiled and said. "Hi." Then she looked back at me and winked. "So missy, how was your *relaxing* weekend?"

I chuckled. "Jaylnn, this is Bryce. Bryce, this is Jaylnn."

"Hey, nice to meet you," Jaylnn said. "You look familiar," slipping her arms through mine then his, we walked together. "I'm Madison's assistant and best friend."

"Well hello Madison's assistant and best friend, Jaylnn."

We all laughed and I looked at him and he returned the look with a wink.

"Here, let me get those bags for you," Bryce offered when we reached the car.

When Bella and Bryce looked at each other, they went into a fit of laughter. Then, we all started laughing.

"Wow, Bryce Stevens," Bella said when she was able to control her laughter. "Is that you all grown up? Is that real hair on your face and not marker?"

Marker?

"Bella, Bella, Bella you finally grew boobs." Bryce stepped to the side and looked at her butt, "and an ass too."

"Give me a hug, you little maggot," Bella said.

I looked at Jaylnn and she was smiling and just shook her head. I pointed to them and she just shrugged her shoulders.

Still hugging and with big smiles on their faces, Bella asked, "Madison, where did you find this creep?"

Still a little stunned, I replied, "In a deli."

We laughed again.

"Bella and I knew each other in high school," Bryce said. "How come we lost touch with each other?"

"I don't know."

"Oh wait," he said in a teasing voice. "You stopped hanging out with me for that ugly, know it all science geek, Scott Graver."

Bella and Jaylnn started to laugh.

"I wonder whatever happened to him?"

"I married him."

"No shit, really?"

"Yep, he's really a nice guy."

"Well," he chuckled, "Then I am happy for you two geeks."

Bella punched his stomach playfully.

"Remember breaking into Professor Buckmen's office?" Bella asked, "to steal the English midterm? We almost got busted on that one."

"Oh, good times."

"We'll have to get drunk again and wrap toilet paper around old smelly wrinkled Martha's house," Bella said. "That was so much fun knocking on her door and hiding to watch her try to get out. She was so pissed, ripping all the toilet paper off her house."

"Is she still alive?"

"I don't think she will ever kick the bucket," Bella said. "I think she has nine lives."

Once again, we all laughed.

"You guys were crazy," I said.

"Best friends crazy. You'll have to give me your number so we can stay in touch."

"Sure," he replied. "Or you can come over to *ClearGrape*, and have a glass of wine with me. I own the winery."

"Wow, you own it? Very nice," Bella said. "I think I stopped there a few time before. I didn't know it was yours."

"I hate to break up all this fun," Jaylnn said, "but we have to get going. Traffic is going to be horrible."

I felt a sudden sadness overcome me. Reality was back. I wouldn't see Bryce. I looked over at Bryce and I could see the same look on his face.

Madison, it will be fine. You're a grown woman and can deal with a few days apart. He is coming next weekend so you will see him then.

"I just have to get my bag from the apartment. I'll meet you outside."

Bryce followed me to the apartment without a word. Once in the door, he grabbed me and kissed me hard. I wanted to cry but didn't.

"We'll see each other in a few days," I said.

"I know," He whispered.

I packed the last few things and zipped up my bag. Looking around to make sure I got everything, I took a mental picture of the apartment thinking it would be perfect to live here.

"What is it, Madison?"

"Nothing, let's go."

"No, what's wrong? Tell me."

"I was just thinking how this place would be perfect to live in."

We just looked at each other for a moment and then we heard Jaylnn's voice.

"Let's go, Madison. The traffic's not going to get any lighter."

Bryce kissed me on the cheek, hugged me, then took my bag as we headed out to the car.

Everyone gave hugs and Bella made me promise to come and use the apartment any time. I kissed Bryce again and got in the car.

"Hey wait. I have something for you," Bryce said. "Pop your trunk."

I popped it as he was running to his truck. I looked in the rearview mirror and saw him carrying a box back. When he got closer I noticed it was a case of wine. He put it in the truck and shut it. Then walked around the car and leaned in.

"Think of me when you're sipping the wine and wearing this." He handed me the button down shirt that I tried to reach for on the bed. I smiled as I slid my fingers over his hand to take it from him.

"You gave me Summer Breeze?"

"A case of it so you won't forget me."

Holding up the shirt, I said, "Never."

"Bye baby. Call me when you get in."

"Bye," I said with a wave as I drove away.

Chapter Fifteen

Jaylnn told me all about the ferry ride and the people getting sick, the elaborate hotel they stayed in, and the items she purchased. Then I told her all about Bryce, the bar fight, and his ex showing up. I left out certain parts like Bryce keeping my panties in his pocket, which he didn't give back, and our lovemaking.

"I can't believe his ex showed up drunk," she said, "Especially on his special night. Do you think she is going to stir up trouble for you and him?"

"He wants nothing to do with her, so I hope not. I doubt very much if she would remember most of the night, she was so plastered. Plus, I think she was doing it for attention."

"Did you and Bryce do it?"

"Jaylnn!"

Laughing, Jaylnn said, "Well, give me details."

"Let's just put it this way. My skin has a glow that will last for a long time and I will be wearing a huge smile for the week. He's coming out Friday night for the weekend."

"Wow, I love your glow and the smile fits you," she said as she pinched my cheek.

Moving my head away laughing, I said, "Stop."

"I knew I saw him before," she said. "But I just couldn't place where until Bella mentioned high school."

"Tell me what you know about him."

"No can do," she replied. "All I know is that they always hung out as friends. I was into my own thing and never really paid attention to what Bella did."

I told her about Mr. Reyes and his wine magazine. Also, how he wants to talk to me about a possible position.

She looked at me and said, "No way, you can't leave *Relax* Magazine. Who's going to run the place?"

"I'm just going to see what he's offering. It's always good to keep your eyes open for new offers. Plus, you know enough to run the department."

"Yes," She answered, "But I can't do the interviews like you do with the clients."

"You'll learn," I said.

"Well if you go, I go. You're not leaving me with Devin and Dylan. No way."

We both laughed and continued talking about the weekend. Well, I mostly listened to her as my mind drifted back to the conversation with Mr. Reyes and the weekend with Bryce.

I dropped Jaylnn off at her place and stopped for a few groceries. After a shower, I put on his shirt that still held his scent. I heated up a frozen dinner, opened a bottle of Summer Breeze and sat on the couch flipping through the channels. I left a message on Bryce's machine saying I was home safe and sound. After another glass of wine, I dozed off for a while and was woken by the phone ringing.

Groggily I answered, "Hello?"

"Hey baby, how are you?"

"Good." I looked at the clock, it was midnight.

"I'm glad you're home safe. Sorry to call so late."

"I had a wonderful weekend."

"Me too, can't wait until Friday. Text me your address."

"I will in the a.m."

"Night, baby."

"Night."

"Madison?"

"Yes?"

"I love you."

"I love you, too."

Chapter Sixteen

Waiting for the elevator at the office, I sent Bryce a text saying good morning, I miss you, and my address.

Donut man was walking towards the elevator swinging his overstuffed bag of grease and sugar. This time, I was smart and waited for the next ride up. I walked over to the newspaper stand and bought a magazine and a pack of peppermint gum. I looked to see if he was gone and the doors closed, so I was safe.

"Good morning, Madison," Devin said as he was right there when I stepped out of the elevator. "I want details. Did you rest honey? Shop? Find a lover? Come on, spill it."

Smiling at Claire as she passed me my messages, I said to Devin, "A woman never tells her secrets."

"Yeah, right," he said as we walked to my office. "Do tell."

"I shopped, relaxed, and went to a wine tasting. It was a wonderful weekend. Where's Jaylnn?"

"In the copy room."

I took out files, my cell, and my laptop from my briefcase and then put them on the side of my desk by the window ledge and noticed it was wet. The ledge and the wall going down to the floor were damp and the rug was wet too.

"Devin, check the plant where you are. Did Claire over water the plants again?"

"No," he said. "The plant is fine. Actually, it needs some water. My window ledge was damp too."

I pulled out a request form and handed it to him. "Here, fill this out and give it to Mr. Sanders."

"Yeah right," he said with an attitude. "Just like the request I put in for the file cabinet drawers to get fixed, so they shut right or what about the one for the hand dryer that's broken in the men's room."

"Just write one out and give it to him."

"Fine!" he said and walked out of the office.

I walked around to the side of my desk and heard a squishing sound. I looked down at my feet and saw water coming out of the rug as I stepped on it. It rained last night but it wasn't raining now. I put a chair over the wet area and wrote out a request form to have it fixed. I brought it over to my boss's office.

I knocked on the open door.

Mr. Sanders was a short, stocky bald man with thick rimmed glasses. He still believed in the old-fashioned bow tie and a ten hour work day.

"Madison," Mr. Sanders said. "Just the person I wanted to see."

"About?" I replied.

"Have a seat. I was about to go over to 'Jenny's Designs Corporation' across the street for a meeting. I need you to go and speak to …"

He was moving paper around his desk trying to look for something.

"Here it is, Peter Miller. He's the owner. He wants to advertise his new line of perfumes in our magazine. This is a good opportunity to sell two pages to him."

"Devin is really good at getting clients to buy," I said. "That's his specialty. Do you want me to ask him?"

"No. He has two clients coming in this afternoon and has to plan for them. I have a phone conference in a half hour so I can't go. I need you to meet with him. Here's the portfolio I have been working on. Look it over and make any changes you want. It's your account now."

His phone rang and he put his finger up for me to wait as he said hello. While he took his call, I opened the portfolio and glanced over his work. No wonder he has a booming magazine, he knows his work. The layouts looked wonderful. Everything was in size order and colorful with nothing too close to each other. There wasn't too much to change except the position of where the bio would be. I can change that on the computer and print out another copy before I go. A contract fell out of the file so I leaned over and picked it up when I felt my chair sink into the floor a little.

Am I losing my mind?

I looked at the floor and it looked fine. I checked the desk legs and then looked at the file cabinet bottoms to see if they were sinking in, but all was well.

I'm going crazy. How old is this building?

"Okay," he said as he hung up the phone. "Does everything look good there?"

"Yes." I tried to press my foot into the floor, but it didn't sink in this time.

I stood up and laid the portfolio on his desk. Pointing to the space in the middle of the layout, I said, "I would like to move the bio space to the top right instead of the middle. I feel that the consumers eyes will go right to the perfume bottle first, which is the selling point and then around the ad for all the history, the scent, manufacturer and where to buy it."

"Perfect," he said. "That's why I hired you. Let me know when you're back and take someone with you."

"Sure. Oh, I wanted to hand you this repair request. There is water leaking in somehow by my window. The window ledge, wall, and rug are wet."

"Okay, put it in the repair file and I will look at it."

I opened the top file draw and slid it in with the others.

"Mr. Sanders, do you want me to call a repair man in to fix all these issues? They are starting to build up in here."

"No. I'll do it. Let me know when you're back."

"I will."

When I got to my desk, Jaylnn was typing away at the computer.

"Hey," I said. "How are you?

"Good. I want to go away again."

We both laughed.

As I pulled out the layout to move the bio space to the right area, I explained to Jaylnn that I needed her to come with me across the street.

"We'll leave soon. I just have to print this out."

Devin walked in and sat on the corner of my desk.

"Let's order Chinese," he said.

"We can when Jaylnn and I get back. Mr. Sanders wants me to go over to Jenny's across the street."

"Oh yeah, good luck," Devin said. "Peter's a hard on."

I looked up from the computer and asked, "You know him?"

"Yep, I tried to get him to open an account with us when he put out his first line of scented powders. He was too cheap to buy a spot with us and he went with a fly by night mail advertising company."

"Well, I'll try my best to leave with a signed contract in my hand."

Chapter Seventeen

My cell phone went off and I turned to get it, but Devin had it in his hands already.

"Oh, who's this calling? Bryce? Bryce who?" He pressed the talk button. "Madison's secretary, how can I help you?"

"Devin!" I yelled, "Give me the phone."

He tossed me the phone and made kissing lips as he walked out.

"Hello," I said.

"Hey there, baby," Bryce said. "Who's that? You have a male secretary? I thought Jaylnn was your assistant?"

"No, that's Devin, the comedian of the department," I laughed.

Chuckling he said, "Oh. I wanted to say good morning to you before your day got crazy."

"Thanks. Did you get my text?"

"Yep, and I already put it into the GPS. Just have to pack a few things Friday and I'll be heading your way."

"All you need is your toothbrush."

In a sexy voice, he said, "Oh baby, something is stirring."

I moaned into the receiver.

"Did you hear anything from Mr. Reyes yet?" he asked.

"Nope. Not yet. I didn't have a chance to look through my messages. I just got in a little while ago."

"Okay, honey. I have two chefs stopping by this morning. I was thinking of adding some sweet treats to go with the dessert wine list."

"Mmm, I wish I was there for the sampling."

"Don't worry, I will arrange for a *private* dessert tasting."

"Oh, baby," I said. "I might spread the dessert all over you."

In a slow and playful voice, he said, "I hope so."

Claire's voice came through the intercom on the desk phone, interrupting our teasing conversation.

"Madison, there's a Mr. Reyes on line two for you."

Clearing my throat, I answered, "Okay, thanks."

"Honey, I have to go."

"I know, I heard. Call me back. Let me know what he said.

"Okay."

"Love you, baby."

"Me too."

I could listen to him say I love you baby, all day long.

I took a breath and pressed the button for line two.

"Hello Mr. Reyes, this is Madison."

"Madison, my dear, how are you?"

"Fine, thank you. Yourself?"

"Fine, fine. I was looking through the magazine you work for and think the pages are well designed."

"Thank you."

"Also, the bio on how the colognes and perfumes were thought of gives the reader a better understanding of how the scent was created."

"Yes," I said. Since adding the history to the ad, our clients' profits have gone up by 40 percent, which of course keeps them wanting to continue their business with *Relax* Magazine."

"That's why I am calling, Madison. I would like to set up a meeting with you and offer you a position with my magazine."

"A position, I have..."

"Yes, I'm sure you're set, but meet me and hear my offer. It will be worth the trip here. I'll be in the office on Friday, is that good for you?"

What should I do? What should I do?

I looked at the calendar and noticed a proofing meeting, but that could be moved to Monday.

"Yes." *If I go there I can see Bryce after.* "How is ten o'clock?"

"Perfect. The address is 452 Parkwire Ave in Mattituck. I'm not far from *ClearGrape.*"

"I'll see you Friday at ten, Mr. Reyes."

"See you then."

"You're not leaving me here alone," Jaylnn said.

We both laughed.

"Come on," I said as I grabbed my pocketbook and the portfolio.

"We have 10 minutes to get there."

Peter Miller was a tall, slender, dark man dressed in a three-piece suit, as if he was going to an affair. He was very polite and made sure we were content with coffee and some cookies. There was not a mean bone in him from what Devin was telling me. After about 45 minutes of giving my presentation and answering questions, he excused himself and walked out of the conference.

Looking at me, Jaylnn asked, "Where did he go?"

I shrugged my shoulders and said, "I don't know, maybe more cookies."

We both smiled and I walked around the table to where all the layouts were and took the one Peter liked and started to write down a few notes on what else he wanted in the ad. Jaylnn cleared the mugs and plates off the table. Peter came into the room and sat down.

I walked back to my seat and asked him, "Can I answer any more questions for you?"

"Just one, where's the contract?"

I could see Jaylnn smiling from the corner of my eye. He read and signed the contract and I made a date with him to do the interview for the bio next week. We packed up and said our goodbyes. As we were heading out of the conference room, there was a loud crash and we felt the building shake.

Jaylnn grabbed my arm as I felt Peter grab mine.

In a very alarmed voice, he asked, "Are you two okay?"

Jaylnn looked around and asked, "What was that?"

"It felt like a tremor!" I replied.

Chapter Eighteen

"Look!" Jaylnn said, pointing to the window.

In a shocked voice Peter said, "Your building!"

I felt my heart stop beating. I ran over and saw clouds of dust billowing out of broken windows and the West wall caved in.

Jaylnn started crying and said, "What's happening?"

Peter was on the phone already with the police department when we heard sirens everywhere from squad cars, fire trucks, and ambulances. A few reporters were gathering information from whoever they can speak to for the five o'clock news.

"Madison! Jaylnn!" Peter said. "We should get out of the building for our safety."

All of a sudden the alarm in the building went off and we all headed to the stairs.

I realized that I might not see my coworkers again. They're like my family and tears filled my eyes. It was hard to see the stairs. I missed a step and started to fall when I felt a hand grab my arm and then around my waist. I didn't know who he was. I looked around for Jaylnn, but I couldn't find her.

Shouting, I called for her. "JAYLNN! JAYLNN!" I was the only one who could hear me yelling because it was all in my head. Everything was happening so fast, and there was so much screaming and commotion.

People were pushing and running in all different directions in the lobby and the doors were being jammed with everyone trying to get out all at once. I caught a glimpse of Jaylnn. She was being pushed through the door and there was no way I could reach her. I noticed a door off to the right of the security desk and saw a few people exiting there. I pushed my way through, going in the opposite direction of everyone and tried to get to the side door. Every step I took, I was pushed back into the frenzy of people. Again, I felt a hand on my arm grabbing it and pulling me. It was Peter.

He yelled, "MADISON, THE SIDE DOOR!"

In a few seconds, we were outside. I ran around to the front trying to see through the dust clouds that were lingering. Pushing my way through the onlookers, I got to one of the fire trucks and I heard my name.

"MADISON!"

I turned and it was Jaylnn. She looked as horrible as I felt. She hugged me and said, "Are you okay? I can't see anything. Madison. What if .."

I pulled her off me to tell her. "Don't think that way."

"Look!" A spectator said. "There's someone."

When I looked over to the building, I yelled, "CLAIRE!"

She climbed over the crumbled wall of bricks and fell to the pavement.

Jaylnn and I ran over and helped her to her feet. She had scrapes all over her arms and face. There was a cut on her neck and bruises forming their colors. Blood was smeared all over her clothes, skin was missing from her knees and she only had one shoe on.

"He, he, h..." Claire said as she fell into my arms.

A paramedic came over and helped carry her to the ambulance.

"Claire," I said to her, "You're going to be alright."

"The..." she said in a whisper. "The floor just went out. He's dead."

My heart stopped and I froze.

"Dead! Who?" I asked.

Claire started to blackout and the two paramedics pushed us aside to tend to her. A breathing mask was placed on her mouth and an IV was being put in her arm and medicine started flowing into the IV and a moment later, Claire started to open her eyes. The EMT's pushed the gurney into the ambulance and they were off.

Jaylnn was leaning against the fire truck. She looked so dazed.

I was walking over to her when I saw a gurney being pushed passed us. A blanket covered a body. I couldn't move and all I could do was stare. Everything went silent and the movement around us was in slow motion when I saw an arm fall out of the blanket and dangle. The silver watch and pinky onyx ring told me it was Mr. Sanders. The tears rolled down my cheek and I felt weak in the knees.

The only thing that kept me up was the sound of Jaylnn's voice.

"Madison," she said. "It's Devin."

I looked where she was pointing and we both ran over and helped him as he stumbled through the broken front door.

We helped him over to a nearby police car and he leaned on it.

He went to take a breath but barely could.

"Dylan," he said. "He was standing." He took another short breath and held his left side. "He was right next to me when…" He was now hunching over a little. "When the floor just gave way." He gasped for air. "And we fell through it."

He bent over in pain holding his side and started to gag.

"It hurts so bad," he said as he tried to stand up but couldn't.

"We need help!" Jaylnn yelled to a fireman passing.

He motioned for another EMT.

"I don't know where anyone is," he said as he started to cough. "It happened so fast." Coughing again and wincing in pain, he continued, "We heard a crack and then that was it. Claire was…" He stopped talking.

"Claire is on her way to the hospital," I told him.

"She had lots of scrapes and cuts," Jaylnn said.

"I'm so dizzy," he said as he moved his other hand to his head.

EMT's came over with a gurney.

"What hospital?" I asked one of the EMT's as he was rolling Devin away.

"Fair Mercy."

I wanted to tell him about Mr. Sanders, but knew he had his own issues right now.

A bunch of firemen were going in and coming out with people, but no Dylan. I didn't know what to do. As another fireman passed us, I grabbed his arm.

"Please!" I said. "There's still a man in there. His name is Dylan. He has blond, curly hair and about 5' 9."

"Okay," he said and was off running into the building.

"Look," I pointed to a broken window on the first floor. "Someone is climbing out."

We ran over thinking it might have been Dylan. It was a man I didn't know. Jaylnn and I tried to help him climb out and his foot hit the broken pane of glass that was still in the frame and it stabbed right into my arm. I screamed but over all the noise and commotion no one heard me. The man was pushing us out of his way and we all lost our balance and he landed on top of me sending the glass further into my arm. I felt the glass cut into my bone and I screamed out in pain and saw stars.

"Madison!" Jaylnn cried. "Get off of her!" She crawled over and started to pull him off of me.

He got to his feet and ran away from the building.

Jaylnn helped me to my feet and an EMT came over to help me to an ambulance.

The tears were running down my cheeks while the EMT stabilized the glass in my arm. A fireman was coming out from where the wall collapsed. He was carrying a body when another crash happened, sending more debris out of the windows, front door and sending the fireman and the body he was carrying over his shoulder, flying into the street. Other firemen ran over to help carry the body and their coworker to the ambulance next to me.

"He's alive!" Jaylnn screamed. "It's Dylan!"

The EMT was putting the breathing mask on him and starting an IV. It didn't look like he was moving.

I yelled, "Dylan!"

Jaylnn held my hand as we looked at each other, then at him. We were waiting to see him move. A minute later, he moved his head and tried to take the mask off. The EMT was checking his vitals when I started to get up.

"Excuse me," the EMT that wrapped my arm up said. "You can't walk around with that glass sticking out of your arm. I have to take you to the hospital."

"Please," I said. "In a second." I walked over to Dylan.

He looked so disoriented. There was dust mixed with blood from cuts all over him. His clothes were torn in a few spots and his shoes were missing. It looked like his nose was broken and his bottom lip was split.

"Dylan," I said when I stepped closer.

He pulled the mask off his mouth just enough to say, and in a weak voice, "It just caved."

Jaylnn came up beside me and reached for his hand. "You'll be fine Dylan."

He looked at her and tried to smile but he was unable to.

Once again taking the mask off he said, "Sanders, I saw him fall right through."

I just looked at him and he knew as he tilted his head and the sadness deepened in his eyes.

In a whisper, he asked, "Devin?"

"He's on his way to the hospital," I said.

The EMT came over that helped me and said, "We have to get you two to the hospital."

"Go with him," Jaylnn said. "I'll follow."

I hopped into the back of the ambulance with Dylan and while we were on our way, I looked into his eyes and saw tears falling.

"You okay over there?" I heard a voice say.

But the pain in my arm that had gone numb before, or I blocked it out when seeing Dylan, was back worse than ever. I heard voices and I think I heard Dylan calling my name when I felt my body turn to jelly and I fell over onto the floor of the ambulance. Before I totally blacked out I heard the EMT say, "She's going into shock!"

Chapter Nineteen

"How long do you think she'll be like this?" Bryce asked.

I know that voice? Hey, say something again.

"It's been four days. Shock can sometimes take a while to subside," the doctor said.

Shock, subside, what does that mean? Who are you?

"Her vitals have been stable for a while now so only time will tell."

I heard a man's voice speaking but it was very hard to recognize who it was.

"She is in shock? Who? Me?"

"Can she hear me if I talk to her?"

"She might. I encourage you to."

I know that voice. What's that sound? Something banged. Oh, that's way too loud. My head, why does it hurt so much? I can't move my body. I feel so tired.

"Hey Bryce, how's she doing? Any changes?"

Bryce?

"I'll check in within the hour," the doctor said as he walked out.

"How are you feeling Jaylnn?" Bryce asked.

Oh that's, wait I know that voice. Why can't I remember who they are? What's wrong with me? Hello, can't you hear me? My head hurts a lot. Please help me! Oh no, it's getting dark again.

***

I blinked a few times before I was able to keep my eyes open. I looked around the dimly lit room and realized I was lying in a hospital bed. My body felt like it weighed a ton and I couldn't move a muscle. My mouth felt like a drought that needs a down pour to happen. I felt something warm wrapped around my hand and I forced my head to turn. Bryce was sitting on a chair leaning over and his hand was wrapped around mine. His head was resting on both our hands and he was sleeping. With every bit of energy I tried to move my hand. It wasn't enough to wake him, so I tried again but all I felt was a painful pulling in my arm.

Why does my arm feel like it's broken? It hurts as bad as my head. I wish it would stop.

I tried again to move my hand.

Bryce, please wake up. It hurts so much.

After what seemed to be forever, I tried again. My hand moved.

"Madison?" Bryce asked as he stood up.

He hugged me and kissed me all over my face. Then, he pressed the call button a few times for the nurse.

I tried to talk, but I couldn't make a sound.

"Don't talk," he said.

A tear dripped from my eye and he wiped it away.

"It's okay baby, you're going to be fine."

The nurse came running in and checked the monitors. She pushed some buttons and looked at me. Smiling, she said, "Welcome back, Madison. I'll get you some ice chips you can wet your mouth with and I will let the doctor know you're awake."

I tried to whisper the words, "What happe…"

"Don't talk," he said. He told me about the building and then I remembered.

Tears filled my eyes again.

He told me all my friends were fine but Sanders died. Also, Devin had broken ribs and stayed in the hospital for a few days. Claire and Dylan were fine and stayed overnight for observation and were released in the morning.

The nurse came back with a cup of ice and said, "She can have a few ice chips. Just a little at a time."

"Okay, thanks," Bryce replied.

Bryce fed me two pieces and then put the cup down. I wanted all of the chips, I was so thirsty. I moved my head in his direction and was able to whisper the word, "ice."

He fed me one more.

"Madison, I thought I lost you. I couldn't live without you."

Forcing out the words, I said, "How did you…"

"Jaylnn called. I was in the car before I hung up with her."

I went to hug him but that pain in my arm was too much and I cried out.

"Don't move baby, You have stitches in your arm."

"Stitches?"

"Jaylnn said both of you were helping a man out of a window and a piece of glass came off and landed in your arm. Then the man pushed both of you out of his way and he fell on you pushing the glass further into your skin until it stabbed into your bone."

I tried to look down at my arm but my head hurt too much.

"You had surgery on your arm. Don't worry. The surgeon said after therapy you'll have full use of it again."

"Well, Madison," the nurse said as she walked in. "I spoke to the doctor and he said you can have some water. I have some Tylenol with codeine for you that will help with the pain." She shot the medicine into the IV and said, "This will help you relax. Try to get some rest." She filled the water pitcher and poured some water into a cup. "Take small sips." She hung my chart back on the wall and walked out.

"Here." Bryce held the straw to my lips and the first sip I took was heaven to my mouth. He gave me one more sip and then put the cup down and walked over to my good arm and moved it gently to my stomach. He laid next to me and wrapped his arm around me.

"Sleep, baby. I'll stay with you."

Chapter Twenty

For the next two months, I took everything nice and slow building my strength back up. The therapy helped a lot and my arm was almost back to normal. Jaylnn looked in on me and Bryce traveled back and forth from my place to the winery. The healing process was slow for everyone.

It was Thursday morning and I thought I better start looking for another job as my funds were dwindling and I'm not sure if *Relax* Magazine would be in business again. I don't want to live in a cardboard box. It was one o'clock in the afternoon and the clouds made the sky look like night. The storm that was rolling in will be a bad one the weatherman said. But it will be a fast moving storm. I thought it would be best to call Mr. Reyes before the storm knocks out the power.

On the fourth ring a man answered.

"*Pressman's Fine Wine* Magazine, good afternoon, how can I help you?"

"Can I please speak with Mr. Reyes?"

"This is he."

He's answering phones?

"Mr. Reyes, this is Madison Taylor."

"Madison dear, yes, how are you?"

"Fine, thank you."

"Are you feeling better? Bryce told me everything thing that happened."

"Yes, I'm feeling so much better and thank you the flower arrangement."

"It was nothing. I'm just glad you're doing better."

In a hurried voice with a hint of frustration, he said, "Oh, hold on. Can you hold a minute?"

"Sure."

I held on for what seemed like more than a minute before he came back on the phone.

"Are you still there, Madison?"

"Yes."

"It's crazy here. So many people are out sick or just took off. I have everyone else answering phones and doing their work, even me. I own the company and I am answering my own phone. Figure that one out."

"Well, there you go. A busy company means more money."

"Yes, very smart analogy. I like the way you think, Madison. I'm hoping you're calling about wanting to come in for a meeting so I can persuade you to work for the magazine."

"Yes, I am."

"Perfect. Oh, hold on again."

Another minute went by.

"Madison," he said. "Are you still there?"

"Yes."

"Is one o'clock good tomorrow? These phones are crazy. I have no idea how they do this all day."

I just laughed and said, "I'll see you at one tomorrow."

"Good."

Then he hung up. I sent a text to Bryce asking if he wanted company for a few days and told him I was meeting Mr. Reyes tomorrow. Then I texted Jaylnn to tell her I was heading out east and if she wants to see Bella for a few days, she can take the ride with me.

I received a text back from both of them within a few minutes. Jaylnn said, "Sure" and Bryce said, "All you need is your toothbrush."

I just smiled and felt warm all over.

Chapter Twenty One

I was just about to go pack a few things when there was a knock on the front door.

"Dylan? Hi."

"I was in the area and hoped you were home."

"Sure, come on in."

"It's nasty out there. The rain has to stop soon or we'll be using boats instead of cars."

We both laughed.

"How are you feeling?"He asked.

"Better." I showed him my arm and the four inch scar that was still healing. "I'll have a permanent reminder."

"A scar is better than not having an arm."

"That's true. How are you feeling?"

"Better. My nose is healed but still sore."

"I have a copy of the report from the building inspector. I thought it would come in handy for when you speak to your lawyer. Did you find one yet?"

"Thanks," I said as I reached for the envelope. "Bryce had his lawyer come to the hospital and I told him what I knew." I tried to call around to get information from everyone at work, but didn't get very far. How did you get the report?"

"I have friends."

I looked at him and he gave me a wink.

"Want some coffee?"

"Sure. Your lawyer is going to want this information, so fax it over as soon as you can."

"Really, tell me what you know." I asked.

We walked into the kitchen and as I made the coffee I told him about the interview I have tomorrow and he told me about his job he is starting in a few days for an accountant.

"I dropped by Devin's last night. His family was over so we really didn't get to talk. I made copies for him too. I called Claire and a few others and I'm waiting for them to get back to me. I heard there were two other people from the office below ours who are still in the hospital but healing and will go home soon."

"Yes," I said as I poured the coffee and put out some donuts. "I heard about them too. I didn't hear of anyone else passing away except Sanders."

"Neither have I." He pointed to the envelope and said, "From the report I handed to you, I think people would want to stomp on Sanders grave."

"Stomp?"

"It says that repair requests were filed and not acted upon. The building was fifty years old and the repairs should have been fixed a long time ago. There were over twenty five request forms for the cracks in the West side of the buildings foundation."

"Twenty five? I could understand one or two but that many?"

"The report from the investigation said because the cracks were never fixed, water seeped in and weakened the drywall behind the bricks. Every time it rained the water would get into the wall, spreading and moving into the wooden flooring causing it to weaken and sag."

"That's what I felt then," I said. "My foot sank into the rug by my desk."

"Yes, it would dry out and then when it rained again the same thing would happen. Over time, the wooden beams and flooring under it finally gave way." Dylan pulled out the report and skimming through the pages and said, "there were fifteen complaints about feeling the floor sag and a few more about seeing water stains on the sidewall and hearing creaking while walking."

He passed me the report, then sat back and sipped his coffee.

"Sander's office was right where it caved in," I said.

"So was Devin's desk, it was just outside Sanders office."

"But how did Claire fall through? The receptionist desk was on the East side."

"She must have been in his office," he said.

"Wait a minute. I was sitting in the chair across from his desk and felt the floor give a little. I thought I was losing my mind. I was handing in a request about the water on the rug that I saw. He told me to file it and he would get it fixed. When I opened the file in the cabinet I saw the requests in the folder. I asked Sanders if he wanted me to call them in. He said he would take care of it. Then he told me about the sales pitch across the street he wanted me to do."

"I would write all that down," Dylan said. "Don't forget times, dates and anything else you remember and fax that over with this. All this could have been avoided if only he would have had the stupid damage fixed."

Dylan slouched in his chair and took a breath.

"How could he have been so stupid?" he asked. "Mr. Sanders was all about work and could care less about anything but making money."

I didn't know what to say. Dylan was venting. He continued.

"Maybe that's why he never married and had no friends. We should get the lawyers together. We are going to get something out of this, Madison. It's not going to be scars or aches and pains to remind us of what happened."

"Sanders died Dylan, and many got hurt. It's not about the money."

"Yeah, but if he had all the repairs fixed, he would be alive and we all would have a job and no marks of injuries. I gave Devin the number to the lawyer. I wrote it down for Claire and others, just in case they don't have one. You can do what you want with all this Madison. Oh, there was another building error."

"Another?"

"Yeah," he reached for the report and fumbled through the pages. "Yes, right here it says, 'the bricks that were still in place at the base of the foundation were stacked on top of each other instead of staggered'."

"Staggered?" I questioned.

"It is when…" he turned the envelope over, picked up a pen off the table and started to draw rectangles next to each other and then continued making the shapes scattered like a pyramid to create a wall. Then next to that wall he drew another one with the rectangles stacked right on top of each other like a column. "See a normal wall is built like this one." He pointed to the pyramid picture. "Where the wall is strong, then you have this one." He pointed to the column wall and said, "Here is where the crack started at the foundation. It kept creeping up the cement in a line, between the columns of bricks allowing water to get in behind the length of the wall. Every time it rained and snowed it weakening the drywall."

We just looked at each other for a minute.

"From being wet and dry so many times," I said. "It couldn't hold any longer."

"Fax this today," he said as he tapped the envelope. "Let me know what you find out. I've got to get going." He stood up and took the last sip from his mug and put it into the sink.

"Thanks for the coffee."

"Thanks for coming over and for the report."

"Anytime."

We hugged at the door and I watched him get into his car and drive away.

I called my lawyer.

Chapter Twenty Two

I woke up feeling better and ready to make a fresh start. I showered, dressed in a blue skirt and tan lace blouse, put a bit of makeup on and pinned up my curls. I texted Jaylnn and told her I would be there by 10. I grabbed my heels, a few granola bars, and headed out the door with my suitcase.

Jaylnn was sitting on her step with her bag at her feet. I laughed when she stood up and was wearing boots, penguin pajama pants and a bright pink halter top with lots of sequins all over it.

"New fashion statement?" I asked as she got in after putting her suitcase in the back.

She opened a granola bar and chomped down on it. "I got my stupid period a week early," she said. "I have no job and I'm out of coffee. How do you want me to dress?"

Scared to answer, I said, "Okay." I looked at her and handed her another granola bar. She snatched it from my hand and stared out the window. "Be glad you got your period and you'll find a new job. Cheer up. I'll treat you to some coffee." I pulled up to the window to Mikes Brew & Bagels and ordered two large coffees and two egg sandwiches.

"Thanks," she said as she sipped the coffee.

"I have to meet Mr. Reyes at one so I will drop you off and meet you later. Maybe we can all go to dinner."

"That sounds good. Sorry for my mood."

"You're allowed to feel like shit once in a while."

She smiled and stared at me.

"What?" I asked.

"Nothing, are you staying with Bryce?"

"Yes."

"Good. Does he have any hot friends?'

We both laughed.

"I need to find someone. I need to get some action."

"Jaylnn!"

"What?" She asked as she looked at me. "I'm human, you know. I have needs."

We laughed again.

I pulled up to Bella's at 11:30, dropped Jaylnn off, and headed to the winery. Bryce left me a message earlier to meet him before I went to the interview.

Mitchell was behind the bar unpacking wine glasses when I walked in.

"Good morning."

"Madison!" he said taking a double look. "How are you? You look better than when I saw you in the hospital."

"Much better and thanks for the flowers."

"No problem. I'm glad you're alright."

Smiling, I asked as I pointed to Bryce's office, "Is he in?"

"Yep."

"Thanks."

His door was open and he was standing next to the window looking over a paper in his hand. He looked so handsome in his jeans, tailored shirt with three buttons opened at the top and his cuffs rolled up. His hair was messy. I guess he never bothered to brush it this morning. He had a five o'clock shadow that made him look hotter and I felt the smile widen on my face.

I just took the next minute and let my eyes absorb every inch of him. Since the collapse, we had not shared each other and I missed him so much. He must have sensed I was there because he slowly turned his head and had a seductive look on his face.

In a sultry voice, he said, "Come here."

I smiled and closed the door, turning slowly so he could see how the skirt hugged my backside. I turned again and with every step I took, I made sure my hips swayed and my breasts bounced just a bit. He leaned back on the file cabinet, put his hand on his chest and took a breath in. When I reached him, he pulled me onto him.

"You're so hot Madison, don't ever forget that. How are you feeling?"

"Perfect."

"Good, because I am going to have you right here on my desk."

Oh Shit.

In less than a minute, I was on top of all his paperwork and my skirt was hiked up to my waist. He moved my panties to the side as he slid right into me.

"I have missed you so," he said.

"Me too."

He took my legs and put them on his shoulders. Watching him move in and out of me made me even hotter.

"Babe," it's all I heard him say before a beautiful moan escaped from him which was followed by my own sound of fulfillment.

All I could do was smile. Then, reality was back when I saw the clock behind him. It was twelve-forty and I had to be at Mr. Reyes in twenty minutes.

"I have to go," I said, climbing off his desk. "I have to go to the interview. How far is it?"

"I'll take you," he said. "Wait, you have one of my statements stuck to your butt." He reached for it and pulled it off.

We both laughed and finished fixing ourselves.

"I know the back roads," he said as he opened the door.

"Want to go to lunch after?" I asked.

"I would love to eat anything with you."

I looked at him and chuckled.

"We can celebrate," he said.

"Celebrate?"

"Getting the job?"

"We'll see first what he's offering."

"Don't worry the job is yours. You'll love Mr. Reyes."

We pulled up to the front door of the building. "You have four minutes to get up to his office."

I leaned over and kissed him and was out of the car running up the steps to the front door.

Chapter Twenty Three

The office was on the third floor of an old art museum which still had various paintings, sculptures and photos of nature scenes displayed on the wall. There were law offices, accountanting offices, and insurance offices on the first and second floors. The whole third floor was *Pressman's Fine Wine* Magazine. I walked in with a minute to spare. The office was very spacious. There was a wall with shelves from the ceiling to the floor that held different wine bottles from around the world. The receptionist's desk was straight across from the display. An attractive redhead was taking a message as I walked up to the desk. She smiled at me and motioned for me to have a seat in the waiting area. I smiled back and headed over to have a seat. One wall was covered with picture frames that held every cover to each magazine they published. It was very impressive.

There were two plush brown couches facing each other and a few floral covered chairs placed on the tapestry fringed rug. Two tall plants decorated the sides of a wide and long window that framed a small sitting garden, which was filled with an assortment of flowers and greenery.

Two men and a lady walked by carrying magazines and layouts and were in a conversation about measurement sizes for an article.

"Hello, you must be Madison Taylor."

Standing, I said, "Yes."

She extended her hand and said, "My name is Chanel. I'm so sorry to keep you waiting."

Shaking her hand, I said, "Pleasure to meet you. I'm sure the phones don't stop ringing."

"I wish they would for five minutes so I could take a breath."

We both laughed.

With a motion of her hand, she said, "Let me show you to Mr. Reyes's office."

As we passed the receptionist desk the phone was ringing again.

"I'll get it Chanel," a short man looking like he was in his late fifties said as he passed the desk.

"Thanks Brett." See they never stop ringing.

"That means business is good," I said.

She brought me down a hallway that had six offices.

"Here we are." She knocked and then I heard Mr. Reyes say, "Come in." She opened the door and stepped aside for me to walk in.

"Thank you," I said.

"Madison," Mr. Reyes said as he walked over and gave me a hug. "I was so upset to hear you were in the hospital."

"Thank you, I am doing much better."

"Mr. Reyes," Chanel said. "Can I pour you coffee or tea?"

"Thanks Chanel, we'll get ours."

Oh let her get my coffee. I never had that done at work before.

"Okay," she said closing the door behind her.

"I'm not sure how you take your coffee," he said, "but here are all the fixings."

"Thank you."

"Don't forget a danish," he said. "It goes great with coffee. The strawberry cheese is my favorite." He reached for a plate and passed it to me.

As I took one, I asked, "How is Mrs. Reyes doing?"

"Oh, the old bat, She's fine."

I just chuckled and took a sip of coffee.

"Listen, Madison," he said. "I would love for you to work for my magazine. I viewed and read your work as you can see," pointing to a pile of Relax magazines. "I thought your idea for adding a bio into the ad was fabulous. I feel with your expertise my magazine would skyrocket."

"Thank you."

"Your work shows your hard effort and I like that. Some offices opened up on the first floor and I am moving the advertising department there. If you take the position, you can hire people for your team. I would like the department up and running in a month. The magazine is covered for the next two months and is in printing as we speak."

Still shocked, but able to answer, I asked, "Is there a team already in progress?"

"Yes. I have two employees working in the department now, Emma and Scarlett. They are from purchasing and have been doubling up on work. Mary was the director, but she left to have her baby, and Jason, he moved into accounting. So now you see why I need to hire a new team. I figured if you were comfortable with the team you had at *Relax*, then maybe they would want to follow you."

Wow, I feel so important right now. I knew I was good at my job, but this is over the top.

"I took the liberty of drawing up a contract which states your salary and you will have an expense account. I will also pay for your move to relocate if you choose to. Look at it later when you are comfortable. I think you will be very pleased."

Holy Shit! He really wants me to join his magazine. He'll pay for my move and give me an expense account. I can have my team from Relax. WOW. Where do I sign?

I was still taking it all in when Chanel's voice came through his intercom.

"Excuse me, Mr. Reyes. I am sorry to interrupt you but you wanted me to let you know when Mr. Phillips from Lars Packaging Supply arrives."

"Yes, thanks. I will be right there. Escort him to the conference room please."

"I will."

"Please take a look at the contract," he said as he stood up and walked over to the counter to retrieve a napkin. "And if you decide you will join our magazine, it will be an honor to have you." He handed me a napkin. "Wrap up that Danish you didn't eat and when you fax back the contract signed, tell me if you liked it."

With a smile and a chuckle, I wrapped the Danish and we both walked to the elevator.

"Enjoy your day," he said as he pressed the button for the elevator. "Please read it tonight and let me know when you can start."

Wow, he is certain I am taking the job.

"Thank you," I said as he walked away.

The doors opened and as I was about to step in, Chanel said, "It was nice to meet you, Madison. I hope to see you again."

"Thank you, nice to meet you, too."

Chapter Twenty Four

If I could have done cartwheels in the elevator I would have. Bryce was leaning against his car when I walked out. He looked so delicious and sexy. He was watching me walking toward him and he smiled.

"So, how did it go?" He asked as he opened the door for me. I told him about everything.

"I can ask Jaylnn, Dylan and Devin if they want to work with me at the *Pressman's Fine Wine* Magazine. "

"You're taking the position?"

"I don't know." Holding up the envelope, I said, "I have to look over the contract."

"He didn't go over it with you?"

"No, he had another meeting to attend to."

"That's Mr. Reyes. He makes his meetings like a social get together, never really about what it is supposed to be."

"So, he told me to look at it tonight and that I would be very happy with the details. Did you know that he has a wall in the lobby with all different wine bottles from all over the world? You would love it."

"I have been to his office a bunch of times and supplied his parties with wine for some years now. Plus he's a friend of the family. He gave me my first vintage bottle opener from 1832 when I took over the winery. That's what gave me the idea to collect them."

"They're very pretty," I said as I sat back in the seat and watched the beauty of nature pass by as he drove. I felt Bryce take my hand into his.

We were waiting at a red light when I leaned over and gave him a passionate kiss.

The car behind us beeped, making us pull away from each other and laugh.

"I have a surprise for you."

"Oh? This is my lucky day. You gave me a surprise this morning on your desk."

"No, not that kind of surprise."

"Bummer, what is it?"

"You'll have to wait," he said. Taking my hand, he kissed the palm. "Mmm, you taste good?"

Laughing, I explained it was the danish Mr. Reyes wanted me to try.

"Leave it to Mr. Reyes."

"He's going to go into sugar shock if he keeps eating all the sweets. Plus, he put four teaspoons of sugar into his coffee and hardly mixed it. It's like he was drinking a pixie stick."

"Ever since I have known him he always had a thing for sweets."

"So, give me a hint on the surprise?" I asked.

"Patience, my dear. You'll see. I have to stop by the winery. Mitchell had a problem with a few of the grape vines and wants me to check them out."

"Problem, what kind?"

"I'm not sure. He said something about mold."

"Mold, that's not a good thing. That could damage the whole vineyard."

With a chuckle, he said, "Not the whole vineyard. There are organic sprays we have that kill mold and we just don't use the grapes from that vine or the ones next to it."

When we got to the winery, there were people enjoying themselves in the tasting room and on the patio. I felt my stomach rumble when I saw a guest nibbling from a cheese platter.

"Want a glass of wine?" he asked.

"Sure."

"Maggie," Bryce called. "Please give Madison anything she wants." Then he gave me a kiss and said, "I'll be back shortly."

"Can I use your office?" I asked holding up the contract.

With a smile, he said, "Definitely."

I could have sworn I saw a gallop in his step.

With a warm smiling face, Maggie asked, "What would you like to try?"

"A glass of Summer Breeze please."

As she poured the wine, she said, "Enjoy." Then she turned to help a customer.

I took the glass and headed to Bryce's office. Once inside, a warm sensation went through me when I looked at his desk with all the papers that were moved around from our hot, wild sex this morning. I walked over to the desk and ran my fingers over the spot where I was spread eagle.

Mmm, we will so have to do that again.

I sat in his chair and opened the envelope. I couldn't believe my eyes when I saw the salary, a hundred thousand a year.

That's twenty thousand more than Relax was paying me.

The work that was listed was the same as *Relax Magazine*, interviewing clients for their bio's, reviewing layout sheets, and handling sales calls. Under the listing was written, 'finalizing the magazine before printing.'

Wow, to finalize the main copy would be a big responsibility. Maybe that's why the salary is high. But why an expense account?

I read further on about vacation, sick, and personal time, and all the normal information about the job description, and then I read that the expense account was for supplies that the office doesn't come with, taking clients out for lunch, business trips, lodging, transportation and food.

Business trips, that'll be nice.

The last page had the moving allowance listed. They will pay for a moving truck, three months rent or mortgage and a plane ticket if coming from out of state.

I'd be a fool not to take this offer.

For the next few minutes, I just stared at the contract and then I took the last sip of wine and signed on the dotted line. Then I wrote a note on a separate piece of paper saying, "The strawberry danish was wonderful. Be careful when I start working there because you will have to share them!" Then I faxed it.

I wanted to text Jaylnn and tell her, but I needed a moment to take in all I read and the salary I will be making. I sat back and closed my eyes and started to imagine my new life here. Then my cell rang.

It was Bryce.

"Hey baby," I said.

"How's the reading going?"

"Good. How's the mold issue?"

"Are you taking the position?"

I didn't want to tell him over the phone that I signed the contract so I told him, "I'm still reading it."

"Okay. Can I ask a favor?"

"Sure."

"There's a test kit in the top draw of the file cabinet by my desk. Can you please bring it to me?"

"Sure."

"I'm half way down the fifth row on the side of the barn."

"Okay, I found it. Be there in a few."

Chapter Twenty Five

I wore the wrong shoes for walking in the vineyard. My heels were sinking in the dirt by the time I got to the beginning of the fifth row. When I headed down the path I saw a blanket on the grass, a basket on top, wine glasses, plates with folded napkins on them, and a vase with flowers. When I reached the blanket, Bryce was pouring wine into the glasses.

In a very low and sultry voice he said as he waved his hand over the whole blanket, "For you, my lady."

I held up the kit and said, "I guess you didn't need this?"

He passed me a glass, clicked it with his, and said, "Nope."

We both laughed and he said, "Have a seat."

Opening the basket he pulled out a few containers of BBQ chicken, coleslaw, rolls, and roasted vegetables.

"Let me help you."

"Nope, just relax and tell me about the contract."

As he prepared the plates, I told him what I was offered.

"Wow," he said. "Moving expenses too. That's great."

"Yes, but it will take some time. I have to find a place to live and then pack everything up. Then there is my mother. She'll flip out because I will be more than just 15 minutes from her."

"She'll be fine," he said as he passed my plate to me. "She'll love it out here and maybe want to visit more. Or move here."

"Maybe. This looks so good. I'm starving."

"Wait. You haven't seen dessert."

With a seductive smile, I said, "I hope it's you for dessert?"

He smiled and took a sip of wine.

While we ate, I told him more about the contract and he told me about an idea he had for adding a catering hall to the winery for affairs.

"The vineyard would be a beautiful background for an affair," I said. "I think that is a wonderful idea."

"It would take about a year to build and staff," he said, as he packed the rest of the food up. "Would you like to help me look at some designs while you're here?"

"I would love to. It will only take a year to build? I would think longer."

He took out a red gift box from the basket and placed it in the middle of us.

While pouring some more wine, he said, "I have some friends that are contractors and owe me a few favors."

"Thank goodness for friends," I said.

"So, I thought..." he said as he opened the box, "that, the first affair could be ours."

I looked at what was sitting in the red box and I felt my heart start to race and I could hardly breathe. I looked at him as he pulled out a chocolate cupcake with a red rose made out of icing. Sitting on top of the rose was the most beautiful emerald cut diamond engagement ring I have ever seen.

"Madison, even though we've known each other for a few moinths now, I feel like it's been years. You have made me so happy and I can't imagine my life without you. Will you make me the happiest man alive and say you'll marry me?"

I couldn't speak. I couldn't move. He took the ring out of the icing and put the cupcake down.

Tears started rolling down my cheeks as he wiped the icing off the bottom of the ring.

He took my hand and slowly slipped the ring on my finger and stopped midway.

No, no don't stop.

He looked at me and said, "Madison, I love you. Will you be mine?"

I couldn't speak so I just nodded my head up and down really fast.

"I'll take that as a big yes."

"YES! YES!"

He finished sliding the ring on my finger and took my face in his hands and placed his lips on mine.

Chapter Twenty Six

I was looking in the three way mirror as the seamstress looked over my wedding gown for any last minute adjustments before I took it home.

Jaylnn jumped up onto the stand I was on, and said, "In two weeks, you're going to get married."

"I know. I can't wait. I'm so happy."

"I can't believe how things change in a year," Jaylnn said. "You're getting married and the profits from *Pressman's Fine Wines* Magazine jumped since you took the job and dragged me with you."

"Dragged you with me?" I asked. "As soon as I said there was a position open you were packed and moved before I got the last word out."

"I know. I couldn't find a job fast enough, so I had to come work with you."

I cocked my head and looked at her in the mirror.

"Okay, okay," Jaylnn said as she stepped down and plopped into the chair next to the mirror. "I missed you and love it here."

We both laughed.

"Are you hungry?" I asked.

"Starving. There's the *Burger Kitchen* across the street. Want to go there?"

"Sure."

After putting the gown in the car, we walked across the street and that's when I got a chill and a horrible feeling that I was being watched. I looked all around, but all seemed to be normal.

Not again! Madison, get a grip. It's all pre-wedding jitters.

"Wow!" Jaylnn said, "This place is packed. Want to get a table? I'll get some burgers."

"Sure, yes."

She just looked at me and then walked to the counter.

I scanned the deck for a table and found one against the railing by the water. I zigzagged my way through and sat down.

Okay, Madison, forget the feeling of being watched, stalked, or whatever. Stay strong and enjoy your day with Jaylnn.

I sat back and felt the warm breeze on my skin and watched two swans float slowly by.

The sound of plates breaking broke my peaceful dazing. I looked over to where the crash occurred and saw a waiter picking up the pieces. I looked for Jaylnn and that's when I froze in my seat. I couldn't believe my eyes. It's happening all over again. Those evil eyes of Stephanie were staring at me.

Jaylnn put her hand on my arm and I almost jumped out of my skin.

"Madison, what is it? You look like you saw a ghost."

"I, I think I saw Stephanie!"

"Stephanie?"

"Yes," I said as I tried looking between people. "She was standing over by the condiments table. Jaylnn, she was looking right at me."

Jaylnn looked back where I was pointing and asked, as she moved her body to try and see, "I thought she went back to Jersey to live with her mom?"

"Bryce said she went back home to stay with her mother and get help."

"Madison," Jaylnn said. "Calm down. You have been going nonstop and you're exhausted since you moved here. With the new job and planning the wedding, maybe it is your subconscious playing tricks on you. You need a break and some rest."

"Why is she back?"

"Maybe it was someone that looks like her. Come on, eat. Your burger is getting cold."

I kept scanning the area as I nibbled on a fry.

"Madison."

"What?"

"Eat."

"Okay, you're probably right. I have been a little on edge."

"A little!"

We both laughed.

When we finished eating, I dumped the trays while Jaylnn went to the bathroom and then I called Bryce. I wanted to hear his voice.

I got his answering machine.

Shit.

I left a message saying I'd be home soon.

With the money that Mr. Reyes gave me for the move and the money that my lawyer was able to get from the insurance company from the *Relax* Magazine case, Bryce and I were able to build a house next to the winery. It wasn't anything big, but it was perfect for us.

"Okay," Jaylnn said as she got into the car. "Where are we going now?"

"I wanted to stop by my Mom's. She was unpacking the last of the moving boxes and found her cake knife serving set and she wants me to have it."

"That would be a wonderful keepsake and a great moment for your Mom to see you use it."

"Yeah, she'll be in tears."

We both smiled.

While I drove to my moms and then to the winery, I couldn't stop thinking about seeing those eyes staring at me. *I know it was Stephanie.*

Chapter Twenty Seven

Bryce was stocking the bar with all different liquor bottles and Mitchell was putting away drinking glasses when Jaylnn and I walked into the hall.

"Hey baby," Bryce said as he walked over and gave me a kiss.

"Look," he pointed.

Jaylnn and Mitchell were saying hello with their lips locked together. We both laughed and walked out of the room for a bit to give them some time alone. They have been dating since she moved here.

"I called the DJ and confirmed everything," he said as we headed towards the kitchen.

"Good."

"I also checked in with Tommy about the menu and he said everything is on schedule."

"Okay."

"What's wrong? He said pulling out the stools for us to sit. "You're very quiet."

"I saw Stephanie. I thought she was in jail?"

"Where did you see her?"

"At the *Burger Kitchen*. She was just staring at me. Jaylnn thinks I'm just stressed out and need a break, but I *know* I saw her."

"Stephanie's mother posted bail and set her up with weekly appointments to see a therapist. Maybe it was someone that looked like her."

"No, I won't ever forget those eyes. I can't get them out of my mind."

He got off his stool and wrapped his arms around me.

He thinks I'm crazy too. Am I?

After a few minutes, he said, "You know what the best two things will be after the wedding?"

I lifted my head to look at him.

"What?"

"You will be Mrs. Bryce Stevens and I am going to make sweet, passionate love to you on our wedding night."

I felt my whole body melt and I pressed my lips onto his.

Our romantic kiss was interrupted when we heard a violent crash of glass. We looked at each other. "Stay here," he said.

I wasn't going to stay by myself so I was right behind him. When we reached the main room, Stephanie was standing holding a gun pointed at us as we entered through the doorway. Bryce and I stopped immediately when we saw her. The mirror on the wall was shattered and the wine bottles from the shelves were smashed and wine spilling on the floor. There was a broken chair on the ground. I could see Mitchell and Jaylnn entering through the patio doors. I was so relieved they were alright.

"STEPHANIE!'" Bryce yelled.

"I thought I could live without you," she said in a very calming voice, "but, nope, I can't."

Mitchell was pushing Jaylnn behind him when Stephanie turned a little to see them standing there. She waved the gun from us to them and back to us.

"Don't move or I'll shoot."

In a very calming voice, Bryce said "Stephanie."

"Don't worry, honey, I won't shoot you because I need you and love you. But that bitch behind you, I have no problem shooting because she's in my way."

"Let's talk about this, Stephanie." Bryce said "We'll have a seat over here. Come and let's have a glass of your favorite wine." Bryce took slow steps and walk behind the counter ignored the broken glass under his footsteps. He passed the register where he pressed the panic button while keeping eye contact the whole time with Stephanie. "Come Stephanie, my darling."

Her face softened and her body relaxed when he called her 'darling'.

"My Stephanie, we can sit here together." Bryce said as he poured wine into two glasses. "Just you and I."

"I always wanted it to be just you and me." Stephanie said. "Can't you see how much I love you?"

"Why don't you put that gun down and we can relax together, just you and I."

"I like the way that sounds. It can always be you and I, Bryce, my love, just Bryce and Stephanie. Doesn't that sound nice? Say it with me."

"Say what with you?"

Stephanie clutched the gun to her chest and said "Oh Bryce, you're so cute and silly. Say our names with me."

Bryce's voice was like a magical spell on Stephanie. She was weakening to him.

"Come, darling." Bryce said as he walked around the counter being very careful with very step he took, keeping his eyes on her and giving her a warm smile.

He placed the wine glasses on the first table where she was standing. With very slow moves, he pulled out a chair for her and said, "Please sit."

Then, just like a light switch, Stephanie took a step back and her face went cold and she raised the gun back up and pointed it to Bryce. My heart pounded ever harder in my chest.

"Why?" Stephanie said. "Why did you look at her?"

Bryce took a step behind the chair to block Stephanie's view to me.

"I didn't, my darling. I was looking at you."

"NO, NO, NO! Your eyes, your eyes went to the side." She stepped to the side and waved the gun to me. "You wanted to see if she is there."

"No darling, I only have eyes for you."

"I can't do this anymore." Stephanie said as she slowly raised the gun to her temple, rocking it back and forth and kept saying, "I can't do this, I can't do this."

I looked past Stephanie to where Jaylnn was standing and saw a police officer creeping around the doorway. He had his gun in his hand and face down. Jaylnn saw the officer, but she didn't move.

"Stephanie, please," Bryce said calmly. "Please put the gun down. There is no reason to ..."

"That's right, Stephanie." A policeman said as he walked passed me, pointing his gun to Stephanie. "Please put your gun down and no one will get hurt."

"Oh great, the police," Stephanie said, "See what you did, Madison," still rocking the gun on her temple, "If you would of never come here all would be fine, but NO, NO, Madison had to fall in love with my Bryce."

Bryce didn't move a muscle. His eyes were focused on Stephanie's.

In a very soft voice, Bryce said "Darling, look at me, I am here for you. Don't worry about everyone else" Bryce moved very slowly to her as he extended his hand. "Please, come to me."

I could see another officer coming up behind Stephanie. Her eyes were locked on Bryce's. It was like they were communicating telepathically.

Just then, she started laughing in a wicked scary way. Her hand started to shake as she pulled it away from her head and that's when the officer grabbed her hand from behind and pointed it up. It went off sending a bullet into the ceiling and all of us got down on the floor. I saw Mitchell covering Jaylnn and Bryce turned to me, but I already got down.

"I have her," the officer said as the gun fell to the floor. He kicked the gun away, pulled her arms behind her back and cuffed her.

Bryce came over and helped me up. "Are you okay?"

"I'm fine, are you alright?"

"Yeah."

We both looked over to Mitchell and Jaylnn. They were getting up off the floor themselves.

Stephanie was being escorted out when she stopped in front of us.

She looked calm, not like she did every other time I saw her.

"I'm sorry," she said. "Take care of..." All of a sudden her eyes went black and cold. She looked mean and full of hatred. "Take care of *my* man." Then in a lower whisper, she leaned into me so only I could hear her. "I'm coming back for him." Then, the officer pulled her away from me and her lips formed into a wicked smile and her eyes narrowed and stayed on me until she was being shoved through the front door.

I thought I was going to faint, but Bryce put his arms around me and said, "She's gone, baby."

After a few hours of taking statements and collecting the bullet and shell, the police and detectives left. Mitchell and Bryce cleaned up and then Bryce brought over a bottle of tequila he had stashed and four shot glasses. We all did a shot without saying anything and hugged each other.

Mitchell took Jaylnn's hand and said, "Come on."

He patted Bryce on his back and said, "See you tomorrow."

"Okay," Bryce answered.

"Night Madison," Jaylnn said as she waved and blew me a kiss.

I waved back as I said, "Good night."

Bryce and I stood in the middle of the room and held each other for what seemed like forever. Then, he slid his hand into mine and said "Let's go home."

Chapter Twenty Eight

One year later

"Hey, Mitchell," Bryce said.

"Yep," Mitchell answered.

"Tell Jaylnn that July 20th is perfect to tie the knot."

"No affairs that day?"

"Only your wedding."

"Great."

"I'm really happy for you."

"Thanks, man."

"Well, it's late," Bryce said, "Let's close and we can finish stocking the bar tomorrow morning."

"Sounds good to me," Mitchell said. "Jaylnn and I are going to meet up with Bella and Scott to get a bite to eat. Why don't you and Madison join us?"

"Thanks, but we're going to have a quiet night together. Put us down for a rain check."

"Okay, have a good one then," Mitchell said.

"Have a great time and tell them I said Hi," Bryce said as they walked out and he locked the door.

"Will do," Mitchell said as he started his truck and drove away.

***

"Hey baby," Bryce said when he opened the front door. "It smells great in here."

"These cravings for chocolate peanut butter cookies are making me crazy," I said. "I can't get enough."

Bryce sat next to me on the couch and lifted my legs on to his lap and said, "Well, you're eating for two now." He rubbed my beach ball sized belly.

"Hey there," Bryce said to my belly "This is your Daddy, I can't wait until you come out."

I rubbed his back as he laid his head on my belly as if he was trying to hear the baby inside.

"You're going to be a great father."

"And you're going to be a great mother."

After a few minutes he asked, "What are you doing with all the wedding pictures out?"

"Making our baby a photo album."

"Here, put this one in." He reached for a picture of him kissing me on the cheek. "This one will show how much I love you."

"You're so sweet honey." I leaned over and kissed his cheek like in the picture.

We both laughed.

"Look," he said, stretching his arm out to the mantle. This picture will look great on the fireplace.

"Oh, I love it ther…" I moved his hand out of the way and stared at the picture in the frame that was already there.

Was I seeing things?

I got off the couch and walked over to the mantel. I picked up the picture frame and couldn't believe my eyes. I quickly looked at all the pictures in the living room. There was something wrong with each one.

In a concerned voice he asked, "Honey what's wrong? You look like your possessed or something."

I ignored him and headed for the stairs.

"Honey?" he called.

I didn't even realize he was right behind me when I stopped immediately in the middle of our bedroom.

"What's wrong?"

I couldn't say anything. I knew my lips were moving. It was like I had no voice.

"Madison, you're scaring me. Is it the baby?"

Then I felt him take the picture frame out of my hand.

I heard him say, "Where's your face? It's missing?"

Then he looked at our wedding picture and said, "Oh shit!"

My head feels funny. I'm going to pass out.

"She was in our house?" he asked.

Time For Me

I tried to reach for him, but he walked towards our wedding picture and said, "That's Stephanie!"

Chapter Twenty Nine

Three Years Later

The sun was just peeking out from behind the vineyard where workers were getting trays ready to start harvesting the grapes. Bryce was looking out of the bedroom window across the field. I walked over, and wrapped the blanket around both of us.

"Mm, morning." I whispered.

"Go back to bed, it's only seven." he said.

"Why are you up so early?" I asked snuggled closer.

"The new shipment of empty wine bottles will be here by eight and I need to check them in."

"Where's Mitchell?" I asked.

"He texted me and we're meeting in twenty minutes to make room in the warehouse."

"I'm so glad you made Mitchell your assistant and hired a new security guard to take his place."

"Yeah, me too. He and Jaylnn are coming over later for a BBQ. I forgot to tell you last night."

"Jaylnn loves BBQ food," I said. "At least twice a week, we would have to order from Zac's BBQ Grill, when we worked at Relax Magazine. I'm really glad they got married."

"Me too."

I walked over to the bed, sat down and said, "Ava is starting kindergarten in a few days and I was thinking of going back to work."

"You want to get back into advertising again?"

"Maybe, or do something different."

He sat down on the chair next to the closet to put his sneakers on.

"Remember the settlement from Relax Magazine?" I asked.

He looked up and said "How could anyone forget the STUPIDITY of your ex-boss for not making the repairs needed, so the building wouldn't have had collapsed and you wouldn't have spent so much time in the hospital."

"Okay that was over six years ago and I am fine now."

I got up and shook out the blanket I had wrapped around me and started to make the bed. "We have some money left from the settlement and I was thinking of opening a small little store. I'm just not sure what kind."

"Wait!" he said. "The barn is almost finished behind the winery and I was going to have wine making classes there, but I can do them in the tasting room on weekend mornings."

I put a big smile on my face and said, "That would be great. I could sell all kinds of things that have to do with wine parties."

He chuckled as he saw me get all giggly over the idea of opening a store. He kissed me and said, "I have plenty of catalogs you can look through. They're in my office. After your mom picks up Ava, come in and I will show you them to you."

As he walked towards the bathroom he asked "When is your mom picking her up? You know she packed her own bag that has more toys and a few clothes."

I walked over to the bathroom, and leaned against the bathroom door frame while he brushed his teeth and said "She's coming in an hour or so and I packed more clothes last night."

We both laughed.

"I'm so excited about the store and I can put Ava on the bus and you can get her off."

"No, I'll put her on the bus and you can take her off."

I looked at him, stood up straight, lifted my hand to my brow, and saluted saying, "Okay, Sir."

He turned around, pinned me against the door frame with his body and said "Oh, you're calling me Sir? I love that."

He kissed my neck and started to lift my satin nightgown.

Ava walked in and said "Mommy" as she climbed on the bed.

He put his head on my shoulder and whispered "SHIT!" in my ear.

I inhaled, let out a long breath of air and then said as I tapped his chest "Tonight, plus I'm sure Mitchell's waiting for you."

He kissed me and closed the bathroom door. I walked over to the bed, put my bathrobe on, and said "How's my princess?"

"I'm hungry." Ava said.

"Me too! Come let's feed our hungry bellies."

Ava laughed as I tickled her stomach, then picked her up off the bed and headed for the door. Then, Bryce's cell phone rang.

"Oh, that might be Mitchell." I put Ava down. "Go put the T.V. on downstairs and I will be right there."

"Okay."

I ran over to Bryce's nightstand to answer his cell phone.

"Hello."

There was no answer.

"Hello." I repeated and again no answer. I looked at the caller ID and unknown was written. I just hung up and went downstairs. As soon as I got to the bottom of the steps his cell rang again and a moment later I, heard Bryce say "Hello" as he was heading downstairs. I was sitting on the couch with Ava when he got to the landing.

"Your phone rang while you were in the bathroom. I answered it and no one was there."

"Yeah, same here." He said as he looked at his phone. "Wrong number, I guess." Bryce walked over to the couch and picked up Ava.

"Come here, monkey. Give me a big hug."

As Ava jumped up into his arms, she said "I'll miss you, Daddy."

"I'll miss you too, but you'll have a great weekend with Grandma and don't eat all her yummy cookies, I want some."

Ava rubbed her belly and said "I'm eating all of them!"

He laughed and kissed Ava as he put her back on the couch and said "Love you cookie monster." Then walked to the door and kissed me on the lips. "See you in a bit."

"Okay, tell Mitchell I said 'Hi'."

I started to close the door when his cell rang again. I heard him say "Hello" twice and then stop to look at his phone.

I stepped onto the patio and yelled "IS EVERYTHING ALRIGHT!?"

He turned around and said "Yeah, no worries."

I watched him walk into the warehouse, and then went back inside.

Time For Me

"Mommy, I want pancakes."
"Okay, I'm making them now."

Chapter Thirty

"Hey." Mitchell said as Bryce walked in. "I'm loading up all the chipped bottles we can't use and misprinted labels into my truck then I'll bring them to the recycling plant. They're taking up too much space." When he didn't get a response, he looked up at Bryce as he taped a box closed and said "Bryce?"

"What?" he answered as he looked at his phone.

"You alright?"

"Yeah, I think I have to get my cell checked, the caller ID is not working. Three calls came in and no one was on the other end and no number came up."

"That's not good" Mitchell said "What if it's a business call and you missed it?"

"Do me a favor and call me. I want to see if your number comes up."

Mitchell called Bryce.

"Yep, number's there. I'll deal with it later."

Both of them worked on making room for the delivery for the next half hour. Then Bryce's cell rang again and he took it out of his pocket and said "Hello, HELLO!"

A woman's voice answered "Bryce?"

"Stephanie!?"

Mitchell stopped taping boxes and looked at Bryce as he walked out of the warehouse

"Yes, it's me. It's been such a long time."

He walked out of the warehouse and headed towards the vineyard as he asked "Why are you calling?

"I've missed you so much."

"Stephanie, get it through your thick skull. I WANT NOTHING TO DO WITH YOU!"

"Oh baby, you don't have to yell at me. We're so good together."

"You stole from me, almost shot Madison and me, destroyed my winery and you think I want you back? YOU'RE OUT OF YOUR MIND!"

"No baby, I got help over the past few years and I'm all better."

"I doubt that."

"Oh please meet me. You'll see you can love me."

"Stephanie, JUST STOP! I WILL NEVER LOVE YOU!"

"But Bry…"

"Go on with your life and STAY OUT OF MINE!"

He hung up and paced back and forth, then headed back to the warehouse. When he walked in, Mitchell looked at him and said "She's calling you?"

He ignored him and asked as he pointed to a group of boxes "Do you know what's in these?"

Mitchell looked at him with a confused look and said "Wine corks! There's a picture on the side and top of the box."

"Well, they have to be moved."

He grabbed the hand truck and started to pile them on.

"Be careful with that one, the top's open." Mitchell warned him.

He didn't hear Mitchell and he tossed the open box on top of the ones he stacked, and it slid off, sending all the wine corks everywhere. He pushed the hand truck over in anger, sending the other boxes flying.

Mitchell jumped back when the hand truck landed a few inches away from him, and said "DUDE!" WHAT THE HELL?"

With an attitude, he said "SORRY!"

"Want to tell me about your conversation with her?" Mitchell asked.

"It's nothing."

"You call pushing a hand truck over and almost hitting me with it, 'nothing'?"

"I'm sorry."

He got up, grabbed the broom and started sweeping up the corks as Mitchell pushed them over to Bryce. After they were done collecting them, the delivery truck backed up to the warehouse doors. "I'll help the driver and you dump the corks and cool off."

"I'm fine!" he said, then took the box and walked toward the garbage.

Mitchell helped the driver unload and stack the six skids of wine bottles. He signed the packing slip and the driver left.

"Are they the right bottles?" Bryce yelled as he was walking back into the warehouse.

"Yep, and they gave us five extra cases free since they screwed up last time."

"Good." he said as he took out one of the bottles from the case Mitchell opened. "They're nice."

"Yep, did she call again? You're holding your phone?"

"No, it's someone interested in renting the hall."

"Okay."

After locking up the warehouse, they walked towards the winery and Mitchell asked, "So, what was the call about with Stephanie."

"She says she's better and wants to meet."

"She's psycho and no matter what help she gets, she'll never be better. You're not meeting her, RIGHT?"

"NO! And I think it was her calling so many times this morning and not saying anything."

"What are you talking about?" Mitchell asked.

"My phone rang while I was in the bathroom and Madison answered but the caller didn't say anything and it rang two other times and nothing. Then it rang again when I was with you and it still said unknown but this time *she* answered."

"What are you going to do? You have to tell Madison."

"NO! I don't want her to know. I'll handle it."

"You ha…"

"MITCHELL, say nothing. I will handle her."

"FINE!"

"Come," pointing to the barn "I'm going to change the barn into a store. Madison wants to sell items that have to do with hosting a wine tasting party."

Mitchell laughed and said "You need wine glasses and a few bottles of wine."

He chuckled and said "That's all *we* need. I think it'll be good for Madison to keep busy with Ava starting school."

"She doesn't want to go back into advertising?" Mitchell asked.

"I'm not sure, but when she talked about a store this morning she was so happy and I'm just going with it. She has the smarts for it."

"You won't have to pay for advertising." Mitchell said

They both laughed as they walked into the barn and looked around.

"The painters will be here this afternoon and by the weekend, we will have the shelves and counters in." Mitchell said.

"Perfect. Madison's mom is picking up Ava and then her and I will sit down and place orders for stuff she'll need."

"Oh, Grandma time?" Mitchell asked.

"Ava is spending a few days with her."

"Nice."

Bryce's phone rang and both of them looked at each other.

"What if it's Stephanie?" Mitchell asked.

He took his phone out of his pocket and looked at the caller ID.

"Shit." he said and sent the call to his voice mail.

Mitchell looked at him and said "What are you going to do?"

He picked up the layouts of the barn that were on a stack of sheetrock and said "I'll be in my office and remember, NOT A WORD" then head out of the warehouse.

Chapter Thirty One

Bryce walked into the winery and went behind the counter to pour a cup of coffee. As he was adding a shot of whiskey, his sister Ann Marie walked in.

"Pour me one while you're at it." she said as she took a seat on a bar stool across from Bryce.

He looked at her and poured coffee and whiskey in a cup and passed it to her.

"Cheers to shitty days." Ann Marie said.

They clicked their cups and took a sip. He spread the layout of the barn on the counter and started marking where shelves were going to be, and then said "What's going on?"

"Three of my workers called in sick and, being Friday, the farm stand is going to be packed and we start apple picking tomorrow."

He took another long sip of his coffee and walked over to the window, as he looked over to the farm stand across the street, he said, "It looks like you have the front of the farm stand covered, but I can send a few of my guys over after they're done gathering the grapes."

"That'll be great, thanks."

He walked back to the counter and refilled his cup with coffee and whiskey. He topped his sister's cup with coffee and then went to add another shot of whiskey but she put her hand up, "Not for me, what's going on with you that you're having whiskey for breakfast?"

Bryce didn't want to explain about Stephanie, so he lied and said "It's just work stuff."

"You need time away, take Madison and go. I'll watch Ava."

"Ava starts school and I want to get back to working. So a vacation will have to wait. Madison wants to do something new and had this idea of selling items for wine tasting parties. I thought I would turn the barn into a store."

"I like that, and it will be great for the winery."

His cell rang and this time the caller ID had a number but no name. He answered hoping it was someone he wanted to talk to. "Hello."

"Please, don't hang up." Stephanie said "I need to talk to you."

"I'm sorry." he said as he looked at Ann Marie. "You have the wrong number" then he hung up.

"Either the whiskey is draining the blood from your face or that wrong number scared the crap out of you."

He looked at her and picked up his cup and took a sip. "I'm fine. What are your talking about?"

I walked in and said "*Where's my coffee?*"

Bryce quickly slipped his phone into his pocket.

"Hey Ann Marie, how are you?" I asked giving her a hugged, then sat I next to her. "Did Bryce tell you about the store?"

"I think it's a great idea."

I reached over, took Bryce's cup and sipped it. My face twinged as I swallowed. "What's in here, alcohol?"

Ann Marie laughed and said "Bryce's special blend."

"Why are you drinking in the morning?" I asked.

"Well, that's my cue." Ann Marie said as she got up and took the last few sips. "Thanks for sending some of your crew. I really appreciate it."

"No problem."

I walked behind the bar and said "I'm worried, it's not like you to drink in the morning."

"It's nothing honey, just work stress."

"You've been stressed a bunch of time with this job and never have whiskey in your coffee."

Then he took me in his arms and kissed me.

"Don't fret your pretty little self over a shot or two in my coffee. It's just something to relax me. I'm not drinking all day."

"Well," I said as I put her arms around his neck. "I can think of a few ways to relax you."

He smiled a little as I kissed him our tongues moved to a slow dance. I couldn't hold back from wanting my husband right there so I moved her hand down to his pants. He broke the kiss and took my hand and pulled me into his office. Once behind his office door, he pushed me against the file cabinet and said "I need you now!"

Pulling at his zipper, I said "Take me!"

He started pulling my jeans down and said "No panties?"

I smiled.

Once he had me out of my jeans, he turned me around, slid his hand up my back and around my neck, tilting my head back to rest on his shoulder. He ran his tongue along my neck then took passionate bites that sent me into grinding movement against him. He wrapped his other arm around me and traveled his fingers under my shirt to free me from my bra. I moaned in pleasure. He bent me over the file cabinet running his hand up and down between my legs feeling my warmth and moisture. Then he slid inside of me. I gripped the sides of the cabinet and push as he pumped. We both continued sharing moans and movement until we tightened and the room was filled with pleasurable cries of satisfaction. He watched me panting and moaning slightly while I was coming down from my high and he rested his head on my back and closed his eye to enjoy the moment when an image of Stephanie's face appeared. He quickly stood up in shock and blinked a few times.

"Oh baby." I said softly as I turned around and kissed him. "That was incredible."

"Yeah." he said as he backed up.

"You okay?" I asked "Did you not enjoy it?"

He just looked at me.

"Bryce?"

"I'm fine. Yes, it was so hot."

He watched me pull my jeans up and then he fixed himself.

"I'm going to the bathroom. You sure you're okay?" I asked as I opened the door.

"Yes." he said as he walked over to his desk and sat down. He put his head in his hands and said to himself, *Shit, this has to end.* Then his cell rang again and he took it out of his pocket and laid it on his desk. It rang a second time as he stared at the number knowing it was Stephanie. Another ring and then he answered "IF YOU DON'T

STOP, CALLING I'M CALLING THE POLICE! WHY CAN'T YOU JUST MOVE ON?"

"I need to see you." Stephanie said. "I'll come to the winery."

He heard commotion in the hallway and quickly said "NO, I'M WARNING YOU. STAY AWAY." Then he hung up as Madison walked in.

"I got one of the cheese platters from the kitchen so we can eat while we shop." I said as I placed it on the desk.

He quickly switched his phone to vibrate and put it into his pocket. Then walked over to the bookshelves, got some of the catalogs and sat next to her.

"Here are two that have wine holders and openers, these have wine tops, charms, serving platters, and these have wine glasses along with wine canteens." He went to hand them to her, but dropped then instead.

"Shit." he said as he bent down to pick them up.

"It's okay, don't get mad because you drop them. Are you sure you're alright? Did you enjoy yourself before?"

He looked up at her and said "It was great." Then got up, put the catalogs on the desk, and turned her chair to face him. He leaned over and gave her a soft kiss.

After two hours of making lists and ordering. Mitchell knocked on the door and walked in.

"Hey Madison, how are you?" he asked and sat in the chair across from Bryce's desk.

"Good, we just placed a bunch of orders for the store and because my husband has connections," I put a hand on his shoulder "..the shipment will be here tomorrow afternoon."

"Wow, nice to have friends." Mitchell said.

They all laughed.

"Okay." I said as she stood up. "I'm off to the store to get stuff for the BBQ."

"Can I come?" Jaylnn asked as she walked in.

"Hey baby." Mitchell said. "Where have you been?"

"Hi everyone." she said as she went over to Mitchell and kissed him. "I was running errands."

"Let's go run another." I said as I leaned over to kiss Bryce.

Jaylnn laughed and said "Come on!"

"Have fun shopping." Mitchell said.

"Always do." I said as we went out the door.

"Let's go see how the harvesting is going." Bryce said as he walked around his desk.

"Okay." Mitchell replied and followed Bryce out the office.

Chapter Thirty Two

"That's the last of everything from outside." Jaylnn said as she dumped rib bones into the garbage. "I can't believe it's so late, but I had fun."

"Yes." I replied. "If Mitchell doesn't stop cheating and sliding cards under the table to Bryce, he's not invited over."

We both laughed.

"We need to make more time to just sit back and hang out. Since Ava was born, the adult conversation stopped or had some sort of child talk mixed in."

Jaylnn chuckled and then said "You'll enjoy the quiet time tomorrow morning when you can sleep in."

"Now that sounds nice."

"I'm really happy that you're going to open a store." she said. "Are you going to hire help?"

I started the dishwasher and wiped around the sink as I said "I do need someone to help me." Then I looked at Jaylnn. "Do you know anyone that might need a job?"

"ME!" she said with smile.

I laughed and said "You're hired. but what about your designing job in the city with the department stores."

"I only have to go into the city twice a week now, for meetings and making sure the window displays are done right. The rest of the designs I can do on the computer at home."

"So, you can help me design the store."

"First thing tomorrow morning, I'm beat." Jaylnn said as she got up. "Come, walk me out."

They both walked to the front porch were Bryce and Mitchell were sipping beers and chatting away.

"Okay handsome." Jaylnn said to Mitchell as she put her hands on his shoulders "It's time to go."

Mitchell stood up and said "It's been real my friends."

Mitchell was getting into his truck when he said as he pointed "There's a light on in the barn."

Bryce looked over to the barn and said "Don't worry, I'll shut it. See you tomorrow."

Mitchell and Jaylnn waved and they pulled away.

"Why do you keep looking back?" Jaylnn asked.

"I thought I saw something by the barn window."

"It's probably the branches and leaves, it's a little windy tonight. You and Bryce should have them trimmed."

"Yea we will."

***

"I'll be right in. I'm gonna shut the light."

In a flirty voice, I said "I'll be in the shower... waiting."

He tapped my ass and said "I'll be back in a flash to get you all soaped up." Then he ran to the barn.

I grabbed a rose out of the vase and ran up the stairs. I pulled the petals off and tossed them all over the bed and a few on the floor leading to the bathroom. I looked out the window over to the barn and it was dark. I hurried and put on my favorite CD, the one he made for me of, love making songs. I then went into the bathroom, lit a candle, undressed, and stepped into the shower feeling the warm water caress my skin. After I wiped the water away from my eyes, the bathroom light went off. I smiled knowing he was coming in and he would wash me with gentle stokes and rubs. I was about to call his name when the shower curtain open quickly and before I had a chance to turn around, I was covered with something and was being pulled out of the shower. I hit the floor hard and then felt a person on top of me. I tried to get out while screaming when something was being pressed against my mouth and wrapped around my head. I stopped moving under the weight trying to breathe through my nose. The weight eased up on my chest but was still heavy on my hips.

I'm being kidnapped, I'm gonna die!

I tried again to get free, but now something was being wrapped around my midsection. As soon as the person was off my hips I started to kick and once again something tightened around my ankles. I couldn't move any part of my body.

"Finally, he'll be mine!" a voice said.

I know that voice, *Stephanie!* All of a sudden, I felt a kick to my side. Tears ran from my eyes.

I heard Stephanie walk around the bedroom making a lot of noise, then it was quiet. I tried hard to free my hands but couldn't. I tried to move my mouth but failed. I was getting light headed and needed air. I tried to slow my breathing and take a few breaths through my nose. Then I heard Bryce yell up the stairs. "I'm locking up down here. I hope you're naked."

All of a sudden, I was being dragged out of the bathroom and pushed into something. I tried to move when her footsteps faded away, but I was stuck.

"Honey, I'm going to wash every inch of you." He said loudly when he got to the top of the stairs.

I could hear his footsteps right by me, so I tried to scream and move but couldn't. The music would drown out any sounds I would make.

Bryce walked into the bathroom and said "The rose petals are a nice touch and I love the candle too." He opened the curtain and looked at his wife all wet. Bryce loved seeing her naked body with her auburn hair all wet sticking to her skin and her curvy backside. He stepped into the tub and traced his finger down her back.

"We're perfect." Stephanie said.

"STEPHANIE!?" he said taking a step back and falling out of the tub hitting his head on the sink.

"Oh baby." she said as she got out of the tub and went to him. "Are you okay? Is your head bleeding?"

Ignoring the pain, he got to his feet quickly, backed up to the wall and found the light switch.

"HOLY SHIT, STEPHAINE!

She dyed her hair to match Madison's and gained some weight. From the back, she looked just like her.

"WHERE'S MADISON!?"

"It's just you and me baby, don't you like my body?"

Bryce put his hand up to his head where he hit it and felt a bump forming. He leaned against the wall, blinking his eyes trying to make some of the blurriness go away.

"Baby, I'll take care of you and make you feel all better." She said pressing her body against his.

Bryce pushed her off of him with force and she landed on the floor. He stumbled out of the bathroom, found his pants, and put them on. He pulled out his cell and called the police.

"911, what's your emergency?" an officer asked.

"THERES A CRAZY PSYCHO IN MY HOUSE TRYING TO KILL ME!"

He opened the two closets in the bedroom looking for Madison.

"Sir, stay on the line with me. What is your Address?"

"42 Nanette Drive, Riverhead"

"Officers are on their way."

"I CAN'T FIND MY WIFE I THINK SHE MIGHT BE DEAD."

"Sir, try and get out of the house and if you can't, hide and DON'T hang up."

"YOU SHOULDN'T HAVE PUSHED ME!" Stephanie yelled.

He turned and saw that she was wearing his shirt and had her hand behind her back.

"Sir, are you still with me?" the officer asked.

Stephanie slowly brought her hand to the front of her holding a carving knife and raised it above her head.

"SHE HAS A KNIFE!" he yelled into the phone.

He threw the phone on the bed and tried to dodge the knife coming at him.

Stephanie missed him and screamed again as she trying to stab him once more, then yelled, "IF I CAN'T HAVE YOU, NO ONE CAN!"

Stepping back two more times and missing the stabs aimed for his stomach, he yelled, "YOU'RE A SICK BITCH!"

He moved his body closer to the bed, knowing the police were listening and recording everything that was being said.

"PUT DOWN THE KNIFE STEPHANIE."

Stephanie looked at him and tilted her head and said "All you had to do was meet me so we could figure out how we can be together again, baby." Then her body tightened and her eyes widened and she continued "BUT NO, YOU JUST DON'T LISTEN!" She lunged at him with the knife and he was able to grab her wrist and back her up to the bed post. He hit her hand against it to knock the knife out. Stephanie screamed and smashed her forehead against his face with enough force sending both of them to the floor by the edge of the bed. Stephanie landed on top of him and she went to stab him again. He grabbed her wrist and banged it hard against the side of the bed a few times again, trying to get her to let it go when he saw a foot sticking out from under the bed.

"MADISON!" He screamed and flung her off of him sending her crashing into the dresser, banging her head.

He looked at Stephanie lying there as he backed away from her and went over to the side of the bed and pulled Madison out. He could hear the police sirens as he was pulling the tape from around her head then he pulled the blanket off so she could breathe.

The police broke in and were coming up the stairs.

Her eyes were wide as she yelled, "WATCH OUT!"

He turned to see Stephanie standing behind him with the knife held in two hands above her head.

"POLICE, PUT DOWN THE KNIFE!" An officer yelled with his gun pointed straight at Stephanie.

"Listen to the officer, Stephanie." Bryce said.

The officer repeated "PUT DOWN THE KNIFE!"

Stephanie raised her arms higher and yelled "NO!" as her arms came down her body jolted when two shots entered her back. She fell to the floor staring at Bryce.

Chapter Thirty Three

Six months later

"Hey baby." Bryce said as he walked into the store and Ava let go of his hand and ran over to Madison.

"What a hug! I think that's the best one ever."

"Mommy, Grandma is taking me shopping and I can't wait to see her new kitten. Can we get a kitten? Please mommy, please."

"A kitten, I don't know."

Ava made a sad face and folded her arms. I looked at Bryce and he just shrugged his shoulders in an 'I don't care' way.

"Well." I said as I put Ava down. "You have the whole weekend to play with Grandma's kitten. Daddy and I will talk about getting one."

Ava's face lit up and she ran over to Bryce and hugged him while saying "Please, please."

"We'll see Ava, come on, we have to get going."

I gave them a kiss and waved as they walked out of the barn.

"So." Jaylnn said as she was stocking bags "A night alone?"

We both laughed. Then Jaylnn sat back on the stool that was behind her and fanned her face with her hand.

"Are you okay?" I asked.

"Yea, I feel like I have no energy, plus I felt sick last night and this morning. I hope I'm not catching a cold."

"I felt that way the other day. I fell asleep at seven watching a DVD with Ava."

"I'm sure any kids DVD can put anyone to sleep." she said.

Once again, they both laughed.

"Oh no!" she covered her mouth and ran to the bathroom.

I watched Jaylnn as she ran to the bathroom and smiled, thinking to myself, *she's not getting sick, she's pregnant.* I wanted to go to the bathroom and tell her but a lady in her late seventies came up to the counter and started to unload her basket which consisted of; four wine glasses, a book on pairing cheese and wine, wine charms and two cheese serving platters.

"It looks like you're having a party." I said as I started ringing up her items.

"Oh no dear, this is for my Granddaughter. She's getting married."

"Well, congratulations then."

"Thank you."

After the lady paid and started to walk away she turned and said "By the way, congratulation to you too."

I looked at the lady and said "For what?"

"You're glowing, darling." Then the lady left.

I stood there and repeated what the lady said "You're glowing?"

Jaylnn came out of the bathroom and sat on the stool and said "I think I just throw up everything in my stomach."

I realized with what the lady meant.

"I'll be right back."

"Where are you going?"

"Be right back."

I ran to my house, unlocked the door and went to the bathroom, and pulled out a box that had two pregnancy tests. I locked up and went back to the barn.

Jaylnn was on the phone when I walked up to the counter. I tapped her on the shoulder and when she looked at me I said in a low voice as I held the box behind her back "Hurry up. I have to talk to you."

"Can you hold a moment please? Thank you." She covered the phone and said "What?"

I stood there bouncing in my shoes. "I have to show you something. Hurry up with the order."

She looked at me as if I was crazy then said into the phone "Sorry about that, what else can I get for you?"

I stood there waiting impatiently for her to get off the phone. As soon as she did I put the pregnancy box in front of her and smiled.

"OH MY GOD!" she said.

I opened the box and gave her one test and I held the other.

"I'm not pregnant." she said.

"You're tired, throwing up and you didn't finish your tuna sandwich, you're pregnant!"

"Did you have to say tuna?" She once again put her hand over her mouth, grabbed the test and ran to the bathroom.

I went over to the kitchen area, took some crackers out of the closet and went back to the counter and sat down. I opened them up and ate one as I pulled up baby names on the computer. A few people walked in and started looking around when she came out of the bathroom with a huge smile on her face.

I looked at her as she walked around the counter and asked "Am I going to be an Aunt?"

She looked at me excitedly as she shook her head up and down saying "YESSS!"

"I'm so happy for you." I said as we hugged.

"Your turn!" she said as she reached for a cracker and smiled.

As I was walking to the bathroom she called out. "They'll be cousins."

I looked back and smiled as she went into the bathroom. I watched the test and the first line appeared but then nothing for the second line. I reached for the towel paper to wrap the test up and throw it away when I notice the second line turning light pink to dark pink. "I'm pregnant!" I said out loud.

I took a picture of the test with my cell and sent it to Bryce. Then threw it away and washed my hands. As soon as I opened the door Jaylnn was standing there.

"Well?"

"They're going to be cousins."

"I'm so happy." she said as we again hugged in excitement.

"Me too!"

"Excuse me, can I get some help?" a man asked while holding some books.

My cell phone rang and Jaylnn said "I'll help him."

"Thanks." I said as I looked at my cell then answered it walking over to the counter.

"Are you ready to be a daddy again?"

"SHIT YEA! You're pregnant?"

"Yep."

"Wow, now we have something to celebrate tonight."

"I also have another surprise for you."

"Twins?"

"Oh My God, NO!"

"You never know. Tell me?"

"You'll know when you get here."

"Tell me, don't make me wait." Bryce pleaded.

"Nope!" I said. "Hurry up."

"I love you, Madison."

"Ditto"

I hung up and closed my eyes for a minute and just smiled.

"Hey." Jaylnn said as she came over to the counter. "I think he's going to buy all our books. Look in his wagon."

I chuckled while saying "You're a good pregnant salesperson."

She laughed.

"Bryce is thrilled. I just told him."

"Is he coming home?" She asked.

"Yep, go tell Mitchell. I got the store."

"Here's your wine decanters you ordered and tell me what?" Mitchell said as he pushed a hand truck full of boxes to the side of the counter.

Jaylnn's smile was from ear to ear. "I'll be right back." she said as she grabbed Mitchell's hand and pulled him towards the barn doors. He looked back and I smiled and waved.

I rang up the mans order for the cookbooks. Then I started unpacking and pricing the wine decanters. While I was making room on the shelves, Bryce came in and said "There's the mother of my children."

I smiled as he walked over and hugged me.

He put his hand on my belly and said "How's my little slugger doing?"

I laughed and said "Oh, it's a boy? Dr. Bryce?"

He laughed. "I'll be your doctor anytime." Then he kissed me on the lips. "What's my other surprise?"

I looked over his shoulder and said "Here comes your surprise."

He turned around and Mitchell and Jaylnn came walking in with huge smiles on their faces.

"What's going on?" he asked as he looked at them.

"I'm going to be a father!" Mitchell announced.

Bryce looked at Madison and Jaylnn and said "Both of you?"

We shook our heads with big smiles on our faces.

Mitchell put his hand on Bryce's should and said "I guess we're going to buy ice cream and pickles for them and beer for us. Congratulations my friend."

Laughing together, he said "Yea, congratulations to you too."

Epilogue

A year in a half later

"Ava, don't run too far away." I said.

"Okay, Mommy."

"The sun is strong for the beginning of May." Jaylnn said as she took off her sweater.

Mitchell sat down next to her on the blanket and said "Mmm, stripping for me?"

I laughed and she said, "That's how our little boy was conceived." As she handed Shawn a small ball and looked at Mitchell, winked and kissed him.

"Yuck." Bryce said as he took Ryan out of the stroller and sat down on the blanket. "Uncle Mitchell and Aunt Jaylnn were kissing, stinky." He tickled Ryan's neck and he giggled, then climbed off of his daddy's lap and sat by Shawn and picked up a rubber car.

I took out the sandwiches, salads, juice boxes, and a bottle of Summer Breeze. I set up everything on the blanket then said "It's so nice taking time away from the real world to enjoy the fresh air and nature."

"Well." Bryce said. "Nature has been good to us with the vineyard last year and so far the dirt looks rich, the roots are taking and the shoots are strong."

"That means plenty of grapes." Mitchell said.

"Yep," I said as I held up my glass "and plenty of wine too."

They all chuckled, clicked their glasses and took sips.

"Look at Ava." Jaylnn said. "She's getting so tall and beautiful."

Bryce got up and walked over to Ava. She was sitting on the top of the slide staring into the vineyard. He climbed the ladder, sat behind her and let his legs hang over the sides of the slide. He wrapped his arms around her waist and said "Hey, princess."

"Hi, Daddy."

"Mommy has lunch all laid out. Let's go have a picnic."

"In a minute," Ava said as she still looked straight ahead.

He tilted his head to look at her and asked "What are you looking at?"

Ava waved toward the field of grapes and Bryce looked over in that direction, but saw nothing.

"Honey, who are you waving at?"

"See, look there Daddy, she has black hair and she's waving."

He looked again but didn't see anyone. "Ava, there's no one there, come, let's go down the slide. I'll race you to Mommy."

"Okay, but I run faster than you."

"I don't think so." He said as they slid down and started to run. Bryce let Ava run ahead as he looked around again. *Gotta love kids.* He thought.

Ava stopped running and turned to her right and stared down a row in the vineyard. He came up to her and asked "Ava, what is it?"

Ava waved, smiled then said "My friend."

Again, he looked, but nothing. He got down on one knee and said "Honey, there's no one there."

"Yes, Daddy, she's going to eat now too, come on." They started to walk when Ava asked "Want to know her name?"

Then Bryce remembered when he was a little boy he had a make believe friend so he said "Sure."

Bryce froze when she said "Stephanie."

About the Author –

Carissa Kopf was born in Brooklyn and raised on Long Island, New York. Her passion for writing started when she attended a literature course at Suffolk Community College and wrote a poem called The Great Wanter, which was published in the Cassandra College Magazine. Carissa enjoys sharing time with family and friends, cooking, drawing, the beach and reading.

After writing the poem, The Great Wanter, she found that she enjoyed the creative writing process. Spending the summers on the east end of Long Island inspired her to write this love and suspense novella. Once she started writing Time For Me, Carissa found the characters came alive and the story developed.

cktfm2011@gmail.com